NEVER TOO LATE

fLiRT

FLIRT

NEVER TOO LATE

A. DESTINY AND RHONDA HELMS

SIMON PULSE

NEW YORK   LONDON   TORONTO   SYDNEY   NEW DELHI

SIMON PULSE

An imprint of Simon & Schuster Children's Publishing Division

1230 Avenue of the Americas, New York, New York 10020

This Simon Pulse paperback edition April 2015

Text copyright © 2014 by Simon & Schuster, Inc.

Cover photograph copyright © 2015 by Adam Burn/Getty Images

For information about special discounts for bulk purchases, please contact Simon & Schuster Special Sales at 1-866-506-1949 or business@simonandschuster.com.

The Simon & Schuster Speakers Bureau can bring authors to your live event. For more information or to book an event contact the Simon & Schuster Speakers Bureau at 1-866-248-3049 or visit our website at www.simonspeakers.com.

Designed by Regina Flath

The text of this book was set in Adobe Caslon Pro.

Manufactured in the United States of America

10 9 8 7 6 5 4 3 2 1

The Library of Congress has cataloged the hardcover edition as follows:

Destiny, A.

  Never too late / A. Destiny and Rhonda Helms.

    p. cm.—(Flirt)

  Summary: Abbey is excited about having a starring role in the annual sophomore class renaissance faire and although her costar, Jason Hardy, has always been a "jerk," she sees him in a new light during their daily rehearsals.

  ISBN 978-1-4424-8403-0 (pbk.)—ISBN 978-1-4424-8404-7 (hardcover)—ISBN 978-1-4424-8405-4 (eBook) [1. Dating (Social customs)—Fiction. 2. High schools—Fiction. 3. Schools—Fiction. 4. Theater—Fiction. 5. Renaissance fairs—Fiction. 6. Friendship—Fiction. 7. Restaurants—Fiction.] I. Helms, Rhonda. II. Title.

  PZ7.D475Nev 2014

  [Fic]—dc23

ISBN 978-1-4814-5188-8 (pbk)

ISBN 978-1-4424-8405-4 (eBook)

Chapter One

ourteen-fifty was a notable year for not only Europe, but for world history. Gutenberg's printing press is considered to be one of the most important inventions ever. If it weren't for that, you wouldn't have these books sitting on your desks." Mrs. Gregory paused. "Now, make sure to write all of this down, folks—there *will* be a quiz on it next week." She swiped her chalk-dusted hand across the black pants on her slim upper thigh and continued scrawling important dates about historical European events across the chalkboard.

I cast a sideways glance at Olivia, who shook her head and rolled her eyes. We were both thinking the same thing. Mrs. Gregory always threatened us with quizzes, but inside that tall, superthin body was a woman with a heart of melted butter. She went easier on us than most of our other teachers did, letting us pair up to study before tests and such.

Still, I took notes. Couldn't take a chance on looking like a slacker right now, not with everything riding on the line.

My big chance.

My stomach flipped and I shoved that thought aside. *Focus.* Surely we'd find out soon enough who got assigned to what positions in the sophomore class's end-of-year Renaissance faire. It was supposed to be today, from all the rumors I'd heard earlier at lunch.

"Mrs. Gregory," Karen said from her seat in the front of the class, thrusting her arm straight into the air. Her hair cascaded like a bright-red waterfall down her back, perfectly flat-ironed and one of my great envies. *Sigh.* What I'd give to not have boring brown hair. "When are we going to find out our parts for the faire? Isn't that supposed to be today?"

Apparently I wasn't the only one distracted during class.

Mrs. Gregory made a big show of glancing up at the clock over the doorway. She pursed her pale-pink lips and tapped her chin. "Hmm. I'm supposed to wait another twenty minutes to release you to the theater. The results will be posted on the double doors." She paused. "But if you're willing to work hard, maybe we can bend that a bit and I'll let class go a few minutes early."

My heart rate picked up to double time, and I nodded as the rest of the class buzzed in excitement around me. The response was unsurprising—most school activities were a little on the lame side, but the sophomore Renaissance faire was the highlight of the end of the year for the whole school, including the upperclassmen.

Even our teachers enjoyed it. Especially the way it brought out the students' competitive sides and made us work together to raise the most money we could for our school. It was tradition for the students to try to trump the year before, and our class was no exception.

As Mrs. Gregory turned back to the board to write faster, mumbling other important Renaissance dates out loud and scrawling key phrases beside them, Olivia slipped me a note. I unfolded it as quietly as I could—Olivia liked to twist and crunch them into the smallest pieces of paper possible—and read quickly.

Are you totally nervous?

"Nervous" wasn't quite the right word to describe my emotions. More like terrifyingly excited. Since waking up this morning, the results of the end-of-faire play auditions were all I could think about. I'd picked my way through breakfast and lunch, trudged from class to class as each minute painfully clicked by.

I just hope I got a good part, I wrote back, crumpling it in a ball and tossing it in her lap. Luckily, Mrs. Gregory didn't really care if we passed notes, so long as we kept it subtle and it didn't distract anyone else. I wouldn't dare try it in another class.

Our teacher talked on and on, continuing to alternate between writing and patting the back of her low bun. I wrote notes without listening while stealing peeks at the people around me. A few were goofing around—mostly guys whispering and elbowing each other. One girl, Liana, was completely asleep in the back, her face buried in the crook of her arm on her desk. Nothing new there—I doubt she'd been awake for the majority of the year. Then my attention caught on Jason Hardy's shrewd brown eyes where he sat in a desk two rows to my left.

He raised one eyebrow at me.

I tore my gaze away, a hot flush crawling up my cheeks. Jason—the bane of my existence. A big pile of arrogance mixed with just enough cuteness to let him get away with treating people like dirt.

Olivia tossed me another note. *He's soooo cute.* Obviously, she'd seen me giving Jason the hairy eye.

Only if you like them tall, dark, and totally obnoxious. I tossed it back to her.

She read it and pursed her lips, shooting me The Look. The one she'd given me since last year that indicated she thought I was judging him too harshly. Frankly, due to what we'd both heard about him, plus my own personal run-in with His Royal Majesty, I felt like I wasn't judging him harshly enough.

Still, I shoved aside my irritation and turned my attention back to my sparse notes. Jason didn't matter right now. I had bigger fish to fry, and I knew that because Olivia had an unrequited crush on him, it was a sensitive area in our friendship. One I'd been careful to respect by avoiding the topic whenever possible.

Mrs. Gregory stepped away from the board and moved to the front of her desk, jumping up to sit on the corner. "Okay, notebooks away. Hurry it up," she added, urgently waving her hands at us. She gave a minute for people to get packed up and finish talking then continued. "As you know, the sophomore Renaissance faire is one of the shining highlights of our school year. We get news coverage from a local station, and even a reporter from the paper comes by. The entire sophomore class participates in this *mandatory* function, including decorating the gym. No one job is more important than anyone else's. All the teachers have consulted with each other and worked together to assign your positions."

A few of the guys in the back groaned, but most of us were engaged and quiet, waiting to hear more.

"Mrs. Gregory," Timothy said from two seats behind me in his slow, easy country drawl—he'd moved to Cleveland in elementary school from Georgia but still hadn't shaken the accent. "What if we don't like what we're assigned to do?"

She gave him a small smile. "Learn to like it." Turning her attention back to the class, she swept her gaze over all of us. "You are being graded on full participation, enthusiasm, and creativity for both days of the faire. You must bring your historical and literary knowledge into your projects or assignments. We expect you to do your best. And, of course, helping the school fund-raise is an added bonus."

I fought the urge to squirm in my seat. Playing it cool was key right now. *Fake it till you make it* was something my mom always said. The decision had already been made, and soon enough I'd be finding out if my audition merited a role in the pinnacle of the faire—our student play.

"Okay, then." Mrs. Gregory gave a big smile and stood. "You're all dismissed. Go straight to the theater to find out your assigned roles. And don't try to skip out," she added loudly above the sudden noise of twenty-five students scrambling for the door. "I'm going there too and will be watching you."

I grabbed my books and tucked them into the crook of my arm. My heart was pounding so hard I could barely think straight. It was silly, getting so nervous about a play. And yet, this could be my chance.

Olivia squeezed my hand, a huge smile on her face. "I'm so excited for you! Let's go!" She practically dragged me into the hallway, her blond curls bouncing with each step. There were clumps of sophomores streaming by us. Apparently other teachers had the same idea as Mrs. Gregory.

The theater felt a thousand miles away, and it didn't help that when we arrived, the place was far too packed for us to reach the doors. Rows upon rows of students were clustered tightly together, and nearly all of them were taller than my barely five-foot height. No way could I get through this crowd or see overtop of it. *The pains of being short*, I thought with a sigh.

"I can't see a thing," I said to Olivia, standing on tiptoes in the futile effort of eyeing the door.

"I have an idea. Stay here." Olivia slipped between two people in front of me and disappeared.

The noise got louder as people talked over each other in excitement, with a few frustrated groans popping in and out of conversations. I overheard snippets, smothering more than a laugh or two behind my hand.

"—wanted to wear a pretty gown, but I have to dress like a serf—"

"Your armor is going to look awesome! Wait until—"

"—*hate* the recorder . . . I haven't played it since fourth grade."

"Abbey!" a voice called out, ringing overtop of everyone else in Olivia's typical commanding fashion. "Oh my God!" Then I saw her push back through the crowd toward me, a huge smile splitting her face. Her brown eyes shone in excitement. "Oh my God," she breathed, "you got it! *You got it!*"

"What did I get?" I asked, trying to speak past the sudden lump in my throat. "Am I in the play?"

Olivia grabbed my arm and dragged me a few feet away from the crowd. "Okay." Her grin grew crooked. "First off, I saw that I'm in charge of the puppet show. How funny is that?" She shook her head. "I barely know how to work a puppet, much less write a show, then make the full cast and create a set. Still, at least it's more fun than peddling turkey legs—sorry, *legges*—to the crowds."

"I'll be happy to help you with the puppet stuff," I replied, giving her a big smile. "It'll be great."

"But that's not the coolest part." She paused, gripping my hand. "You got the lead, Abbey. You're the female star of the play.

In addition to now helping me with the puppets, of course," she added with a wink.

A big squeal bubbled out of me before I could stop it. "Oh, wow!" I reached over to hug her. "This is the best day ever!" In my gut I'd felt my audition was good enough to warrant me a speaking part . . . but never could I have dreamed I'd get the lead. That was reserved for the upper clique, people like Karen, who achieved every accolade possible in school.

The play was a Renaissance-era romantic comedy, pitting two brothers against each other as they tried to win the hand of their childhood friend Rosalyn.

My character. The lead female.

The realization was overwhelming, thrilling, and I squeezed Olivia harder.

Olivia pulled back, her smile wobbling a little. She put her hands on my shoulders, glancing down then flicking her gaze back up to me.

"What's wrong?" I asked.

"Um, there's one other thing. I think it's great news, but you might not be so thrilled." She swallowed. "Don't shoot the messenger, okay?"

Somehow I knew what she was going to tell me; something in my gut had a nasty feeling. Still, I had to hear it from her to confirm. "What is it?"

"Well . . . Jason Hardy got the part of the male lead."

Leave it to him to ruin the happiest moment of my entire

sophomore year. I heaved a large sigh, the wind sapped from my sails.

Olivia dropped her arms, her face going flat in an instant. "Come on, now. Don't be like that."

"I don't want to get into this right now," I said as quietly as I could. Which was hard, considering the surge of irritation boiling in me. "Let's get out of here."

We made our way to our lockers then met at the back door of the school a few minutes later. The early May air was balmy and warm, a refreshing change from being trapped in our stale school and the typical Cleveland-area rainy spring. Buds erupted and blossomed into bold-colored flowers on the green-leafed trees lining our path to my house. Birds chirped and danced along the sidewalk, bouncing on tiny feet and pecking at spots on the ground.

A gorgeous afternoon . . . but it wasn't enough to make me feel better.

I shouldered my bag higher.

"I can tell you're not happy," Olivia said, her footsteps in perfect rhythm with mine—an old habit we'd started in middle school when walking back and forth every day. "But you should be. Even if you don't like Jason, this will force you to give him a chance and see him in a new light."

"But I don't want to." I crossed the street, knowing I sounded petulant but unable to resist adding, "And actually, I *did* give him the benefit of the doubt before—this is where it got me."

"I can't believe you're still upset over that. It was last year." Olivia sighed. "He's different. Yes, I know he was a jerk before, but he's not like that anymore." Her voice took a soft edge that drilled back into my head about how big her crush was growing.

It was that crush that kept me from spouting off about all the ways Jason was awful. The many, many, *many* ways. Instead, I bit my tongue, for the sake of my best friend, and we made our way back to my house.

Why am I letting him steal my moment? That sudden thought jarred me. I straightened my spine as I keyed the lock to my house. Jason might put a damper on this moment, but I deserved to celebrate my success. I wasn't going to let him take that from me.

"We need ice cream," I declared, heading right into the kitchen as she dumped her bag on our living room sofa. "To celebrate the start of a successful Renaissance faire."

I was determined to make this the best play, the best *faire*, the school had ever seen.

Chapter ☙ Two

"Abbey! Dinner's ready!" My mom's voice rang clearly from downstairs in the kitchen over the soft melody of my violin.

I still had another fifteen minutes of practice to do later, not that my rehearsal was any good today. I was far too distracted by the faire news, so I was missing notes left and right. Yeesh. This was so unlike me.

I put the bow and instrument back in their case and shuffled down our tan carpeted stairs. "Coming," I replied, weaving through the hallway, living room, into our kitchen.

My mom greeted me at the kitchen entry, planting a small kiss on my cheek. Her thick light-brown hair was tied at the nape into a ponytail, and with the barely present lines on her face and light makeup, she almost looked more like an older sister than a mom. "Can you please set the table? Don's home early, so he's going to be joining us."

As if on cue, my stepdad walked in. "Hey, kiddo," he said, giving me a fake slug in the arm. "Need some help?"

"Help would be awesome," I told him, giving a swift hug. "Hope you had a good day at the office."

With two hands, the table was set quickly and food laid out in a lovely display of roasted turkey breasts, homemade mashed potatoes, dinner rolls, and my favorite, baked mac and cheese.

My older sister, Caroline, finally slipped in—as typical, right after everything was already done—and took her seat across from me. "I'm starving," she groaned, flopping so her head rested on the back of her seat. Her dark-blond hair draped casually over her brow, looking effortlessly chic in spite of the messiness. "School was *so* hard today, and the homework never ends. I thought this year was supposed to be easier."

"Cheer up," Don said with a chuckle, offering her the bowl of rolls. "At least it's almost over. Then you can start college and enjoy those seven a.m. classes. Can't say I miss those."

"Hardy har," she mumbled back to him, though I did see her mouth twist in a half smile.

My news bubbled right beneath my skin, bursting to get free. I waited until Mom took her seat then blurted out, "I got the lead in the Renaissance faire play!"

Caroline blinked and looked over at me, her green eyes growing wide. Since she was a senior and had participated in the faire two years ago, she knew what a coup this was to me. "Congrats," she said, giving me a genuine grin. "That's no small thing."

Her praise warmed me. "Thanks."

Then her left eyebrow rose wickedly. "But it won't beat our class—last year's didn't come close to matching what we did."

I stuck my tongue out at her, but in a way she was right. This year's juniors had tried, but not much could trump the acts the seniors had done. They had a gypsy troupe wandering through the gym's "grounds," doing fun interactive dances, swallowing fire (to the principal's surprise and horror, I was sure), and telling fortunes. I wish I'd been able to see it, but I was only in eighth grade at the time, and the faire was held during school hours. "Just wait until you see what we have planned," I told her. Not that we'd planned anything yet, but the play sounded fun from what I'd read, and our class was quite creative. It would turn out wonderfully, I just knew it.

"I'm sure it'll be lovely," my mother said, spooning a large hunk of mashed potatoes onto her plate and shooting me a smile. "I'll make certain that Don and I take off work so we can attend."

I beamed at her. "Thanks, Mom."

Dinner went fast. After helping to load the dishwasher, I flew back up to my room to finish practicing violin. Music was one of my biggest passions; practice was never just practice, never just boring duties. Usually I was able to lose myself in a song, my fingers flying across the thin strings, the light vibrato of my bow drawing out and sustaining the notes in a sweet, melodic tone.

But not today. The stain of Jason tainting my perfect moment wouldn't let me go, adding to my distraction about the play. The music was flat in my ear, the notes not quite in tune. Frustrated, I dropped the violin and bow on my bed.

My mind flew instantly back to last year and the freshman homecoming dance. My first official high school event. Olivia and I had been so excited, taking a full two hours to do our makeup and hair. Our shopping expedition to find the perfect dresses and shoes was quite a quest, but that night we looked perfect. My dress was bold red, a bright slash of color in a sea of tight black gowns.

I'd been proud of standing out, being different than the others.

Olivia and I had spent the first hour dancing our feet sore, laughing and having the best time ever. No guys had asked us to dance, but that was okay, because we had each other. Besides, we were still new to the school and more than a little intimidated by everyone else.

I dug my fingers into the bedspread, vividly remembering the way I'd felt when I'd overheard The Conversation in the gym on the way back from the bathroom:

Random friend of Jason's: "Gonna ask anyone to dance?"

Jason, looking around but not seeing me, slightly behind him: "Nah. I don't like to dance at these things. It makes me look stupid."

Friend: "Slow dancing is different, though." Pause. "What

about one of those cute girls? Like those two who are always together—Olivia and . . . Alley?"

My face instantly flamed. I knew he was talking about me, even if he'd messed my name up.

Jason, laughing. "Who, Abbey? *Right*. Only if I want to be bored to death. There's nothing interesting about her at all."

Somehow I'd managed to make my feet move, marched right by both of them with my head held high. I refused to let Jason see me embarrassed and would not give him the pleasure of showing my emotions. But that hot flood of mortification slid through me, and the second I got home later that night, I cried.

Nice guy, huh. He might have fooled Olivia into thinking he'd changed, but not me. I wouldn't forgive him, and I wouldn't forget.

I'd spent most of this year patently ignoring him in class, pretending like he didn't exist. No eye contact, no conversations, no engagement at all. And now I had to work opposite of him several days a week over the next few weeks, drilling lines over and over again. Pretending we were in love onstage.

Could I really do this? Would my acting skills be strong enough to help me swallow my revulsion at his utter snobbery and fake my way through it?

Well, there was no way I was letting him ruin this for me. If I was serious about the arts, it had to start now. Artists and musicians didn't let personal feelings get in the way of a performance. They channeled that emotion, twisted it into something usable.

I could do the same.

And maybe if I kept telling myself that, I'd eventually believe it.

There was nothing worse than gym at 7:45 in the morning.

Mrs. Belati's shrill whistle pierced my ears, and I shivered in the light chill of the crisp morning air. "Come on, ladies! Let's get some hustle going—the guys are beating you in lap times!" She jogged over to talk to a group of girls behind me, her green vinyl pants *vip-vipping* with each step.

"This stinks," my friend Lauretta whispered. She tucked a strand of pink-tipped hair behind her ear from where it had slid out of her ponytail and stepped up her pace. "How can she be so perky this early?"

I groaned and walked faster beside Lauretta, shivering lightly. Shouldn't mornings be warmer in May by now? "I have no idea."

"Ladies, I want to see you running, not walking and talking," Mrs. Belati said to Lauretta and me, popping up right behind us. "You're getting smoked by the boys today. Move it, move it!"

A snicker came from my left side right as someone blurred by me. Jason. He waggled his fingers at Lauretta and me as he passed by, following the curve of the path up ahead in a smoothly paced gait. A natural runner, it seemed. Absurdly gifted at everything from school to acting to sports.

What a shocker.

My cheeks burned from irritation, and suddenly I felt over-heated and flushed all over. The urge to beat him came over me in a sharp rush. "Oh, it's on," I whispered. "Lauretta, I'll see ya at the end."

"Go, girl!" she said, rooting me on.

I kicked up my pace and whipped around the corner, coming right up behind him. My lungs started to ache but I ignored it, focused on putting one foot in front of the other, keeping Jason in my sights the whole time.

Inching closer, closer . . .

My thighs trembled slightly as I made it to his side, our feet slapping in rhythm on the concrete path. He glanced over at me, blinking in surprise. Then he shot me a small, crooked grin and pushed ahead.

Oh, no you don't. I made myself go faster, harder. The space under my ribs started to scream for relief. *Come on, Abbey*, I pleaded with myself. *Do this.*

Cheers erupted from all around us. The girls were rooting me on. The guys were shouting for Jason to beat me. A speedy peek over my shoulder confirmed that even Mrs. Belati watched our race with interest.

The finish line loomed ahead. Just one more curve, and it was a straight path to winning. I could do this. I could do it.

"Wow," Jason said on a breath, his arms sawing by his sides as a couple of beads of sweat trailed down his face. "You're fast."

A small swell of pride hit me at the acknowledgment, but I shoved it aside. *Focus.*

We hit the curve, neck and neck.

Then I edged out slightly in front.

Finally!

But he was still too close. So close that I could hear the soft, shallow puffs of his breath—he was panting as hard as I was. My right side began to throb and stab in pain and my legs shook even harder.

Thirty feet from the finish, Jason must have gotten a last burst of energy. He evened up to my side for a moment then pushed ahead and beat me, crossing the white line with less than a second to spare.

Defeat dampened me in a swift rush, and I slowed to a crawl, slumped over and lungs desperately gasping for air. I couldn't believe I'd lost to him. So much for beating the arrogant—

"That was an awesome run," Jason said in between breaths, clapping me on the back. Sweat now fully dribbled down his flushed face, plastering the strands along his hairline to his forehead. He wore a huge grin, his straight white teeth flashing. "Nice job."

I blinked, stood up to look at him, the stitch in my side temporarily forgotten. Did Jason Hardy just compliment me? And touch me?

What planet was this?

"Uh, thanks," I finally muttered, unsure how else to respond and too stunned to think of something more coherent to say.

He nodded then strolled away, back to his group of friends.

"Well done!" Mrs. Belati said loudly with a few hearty claps before she blew her whistle again. "Okay, everyone. Show's over—let's work on stretches and wrap up class for the day."

"That was amazing," Lauretta said, admiration shining in her voice and her eyes. She slipped beside me as we made our way to the middle of the field. "You were unbelievably fast." She elbowed me in the side. "You've been holding out on us, lady."

"Oh, please," I said with a laugh, lungs still burning for air as I tried to play it cool. "It was just a silly run."

"Not so silly to him," she retorted, nudging her chin toward Jason. "He seemed impressed." She gave a small sigh, eyeing him while he bent over and stretched his calves.

Oh, no. Not her, too. Did everyone in the school have a crush on him? Okay, I'd give him that he was undeniably cute. His answers in World History showed me he was reasonably intelligent and could maintain a conversation, as well, so I had to admit that he wasn't a dummy.

And since I was being honest, I could also recognize that he didn't make me feel like a total loser just now when I lost our race.

I drew in slow breaths and began my stretches, forcing myself to keep from looking over at Jason. Just because he had one isolated flare-up of being nice to me didn't mean that was who he really was. It didn't mean that I could expect kindness from him on a regular basis.

And if I wanted to get through this play with my pride intact, I had to remember that.

Chapter ◉ Three

Abbey!" A low, rumbling voice stopped me dead in my tracks. Robert, head of the yearbook committee, newspaper editor in chief, chess team captain, and all-around busy guy, was bellowing for me from about fifty feet away. "Hold up—I need to talk to you for a second!"

I moved over to the side of the hallway, propping my notebook on my hip. "What's going on?"

He strolled toward me on long, gangly legs, his gray T-shirt half-tucked into his jeans. "Do you have time to talk?" His black hair was a messy mop, looking like he'd run his fingers through it constantly. Typical Robert.

I glanced at my cell: three fifty. Only ten minutes until our first gathering for the play, and I didn't want to be late. "Well,

I can spare a minute or two, but then I have to run. What's going on?"

"We need your help," Robert said, shoving his glasses up his nose. "Our newspaper photographer took some pictures of the spring sports teams last week, but her computer crashed and she lost all of her shots."

"You want *me* to take pictures?" I raised one eyebrow but was kind of intrigued. I enjoyed amateur photography and had taken art class last year with Robert. My end-of-year project was a series of black-and-white nature shots, something he'd actually complimented me on, saying I had a great eye for composition.

"She doesn't have the time to go back and redo them, since we still need other photos and we're on a time crunch." He dug into his back pocket and handed me a piece of paper, giving an apologetic shrug. "Sorry, I was writing it in a hurry, so my handwriting is a little messy. It's not a lot, but we'd appreciate it."

"Sure. I'll help." I glanced over the list:

Baseball—practice shots are fine

Softball—practice shots

Golf (boys and girls)—need to get game shots

Soccer—can do practice shots

Should be easy enough. The golf course was fairly close to my house, so I could easily walk there. And the rest I could do after school on the grounds. "E-mail me later with specifics, like how many shots and when they're due, okay?" I grabbed the black pen tucked in the spiral of my notebook, wrote my e-mail on the bottom of the paper, ripped it off, and gave it to him. "I have to go to play practice, but we can talk later."

"Thank you!" He gave me a toothy grin. "You just saved my hide."

I nodded then took off back down the hallway, my tennis shoes padding across the tiled floor. Nerves flooded me once again, shaking my hands.

You can do this. You can do this.

Don always said that success started in the mind. Staying calm and in control was my best strategy. I practiced some relaxation techniques and controlled my breathing in slow, measured inhales and exhales as I neared the theater, where we'd be doing our rehearsals.

I passed through the double doors and moved down the aisle; there were a dozen people already waiting in seats in the front row. Surprisingly enough, Liana—the World History snoozer—was there too, her head dipped back on the seat as she stared blindly at the ceiling.

Interesting. How had I missed her audition? And what role did she have? Was it onstage, or backstage?

"Oh good, we're all here," Mr. Ferrell said as he popped out from behind the curtains and made his way to the front of the stage, holding a clipboard. He sat down on the edge, legs dangling. His jeans were faded, and he had on a flannel shirt lightly fitted and worn. His brown hair was lightly mussed, with black-rimmed glasses pushed back on top of his head.

He was definitely one of the cutest teachers in our school—in his early twenties and still single, from what we'd heard. I dropped into a seat and smothered a laugh behind my hand as the girls around me sat up, inconspicuously fluffing their hair and straightening their shirts.

Mr. Ferrell, utterly clueless about how many girls found him attractive, grabbed the clipboard and absently flipped through the top few pages. "Okay, I have our rehearsal schedules here. All practices will be after school, twice a week until the week before the play, when we'll rehearse three times a week. The day before the play will be a full-costume rehearsal. . . ." With this, he looked up and winked. "We gotta give you ladies a chance to get used to wearing those dresses, right?"

A few high giggles smattered throughout the theater.

"And I'll be giving you the scripts today too. Now, where are my leads?" He scanned the audience, his eyes connecting with mine. "Ah, good. I see our heroine. And our male lead is . . ."

In the front row, an arm shot up and waved.

"Jason. Gotcha. Aaaaand I see our two understudies, as well." Mr. Ferrell slid off the stage and walked around to hand out the schedules to us, then went to the left of the stage, where there was a beat-up cardboard box. He heaved it to center stage then plopped it down. "Well, that's all I have for our meeting today, folks. When you leave, grab one of these scripts and start reading tonight, please. Time is of the essence, and while the play isn't long, it's important for you to start memorizing your lines. We're going to start blocking the opening scenes this week. And please note that all practices are mandatory—you need to be here."

I headed over to dig through the box and take a copy. The play itself wasn't going to be very lengthy, maybe an hour from the looks of it, but the title—*All's Fair in Love*—promised some fun and witty dialogue, as well as the love-triangle plot. I couldn't wait to start.

As I made my way back down the aisle to gather my notebook, I heard a deep voice say, "Abbey, wait."

I froze in place. We'd already had an encounter earlier today . . . it figured that wouldn't be enough. With a light sigh, I turned and faced Jason. "Yes?"

He sauntered up to me, taking his time like he didn't have a care in the world. Probably didn't—guys like that had nothing to worry about. He gave me a casual one-shoulder shrug. "I was thinking, you and I should probably schedule some extra rehearsal times to make sure things are progressing at the right pace."

Instantly, I bristled. What, did he think I was going to ruin this or something? It was bad enough that I had to sit in World History with him, be in gym with him, and practice with him twice a week. Now he wanted to throw in some extra torture sessions just for kicks. "You don't think we'll get it all down with our regular practices?"

"It just needs to be perfect." A thread of irritation pierced his words, and he furrowed his brow.

"It will be perfect. You don't need to worry about me," I

retorted. "I won't have any problems keeping up." A lot of bravado, I knew, but he was setting me on edge, and I felt a sudden need to prove myself worthy of a role I'd already won.

His mouth went flat. "I won't have any problems with it either. It was just an idea, you know."

At his words, my stomach pinched. For as much as he bugged me, as much as I was rightfully angry at his snobbery, it was me being the pain in the backside right now. "Well, it was a good idea," I made myself admit. "Maybe we can squeeze in a few extra practices. Just to be on the safe side."

Jason gave me a quick nod, his eyes unreadable. He dug a pen out of his pocket, grabbed my hand, and flipped it over, palm up. I blinked, confused, my skin tingling where his fingers brushed my bare skin.

He slid my sleeve up, baring my wrist and forearm. "Here's my cell," he said, writing his phone number on my arm. The pen tickled as it slid across my skin. "Text or call me with your schedule of when you're free so we can work it out."

My heart gave a strange, painful thud, and I swallowed and nodded.

He clicked the tip of the pen back into itself then looked up at me as he crammed the pen back into his pocket. His eyes were deep, strangely intense and open, and for a moment I forgot how much I disliked him.

After a few seconds he gave me a toothy grin and chuckled. "As tempting as it must be to keep my number on you, make sure you wash that arm later. Don't want anyone getting the wrong idea."

I rolled my eyes, jerked my hand away, and shoved the sleeve back down. Then I grabbed my stuff and booked it out the theater without looking back, trying to force back the strange, swirling emotions I'd had when he'd touched me.

Jason was a jerk. Arrogant and full of himself. Of course he didn't even bother to ask for my number—he just gave me his, expecting me to be the one to reach out to him. Writing it on my skin, too.

By the time I made it outside, I'd almost forgotten how it had felt when his thumb had brushed against my pulse point.

Almost.

Rosalyn: Wait, you . . . you love me? But how can this be? You have done nothing but tease and torture me from childhood on. Our whole history is built upon this strange antagonism between us.

William: From the first time I pulled your hair at the side of the river, I knew I loved you. How could I not? Especially when you returned my attention with a punch in the nose—well deserved, I might add.

Rosalyn: I never knew you felt that way. Why did you not speak of these feelings before . . . before your brother made his intentions clear toward me?

William (stepping closer, taking Rosalyn's hand): Would you

have trusted me, had you known? I have railed against
this for far too long, believe me. My heart did struggle
with the knowledge that I could not let my brother win
your hand. Not when . . . when I wanted it for my own.
I could no longer remain silent.
Rosalyn (closing the gap between them): Oh, my dear
William, I love you too.
They kiss.

Wait, what?

I blinked and reread that last line, jaw dropped. That couldn't
be right. But there it was, black letters on white paper, taunting me.

I was going to have to kiss Jason Hardy. On the mouth and
everything.

Well duh, Abbey.

My hand shook as I pushed up my sleeve, staring at the
numbers I'd made myself ignore through dinner, two hours of
homework, and yet another distracted violin practice. But still I
felt branded, unable to shake off the memory of his warm fingers
pressing on my skin.

And now, thanks to the play, we were going to have to press
our lips together too. How could I do it?

How could Jason Hardy be my first *real* kiss?

My cheeks burned with embarrassment. I'd been saving my
first kiss for someone special, a guy worth waiting for. I hadn't
found him yet, but it didn't mean he wasn't out there, looking for

me too. All this time, and now it didn't matter. It was going to be wasted on a total jerk.

Maybe I could ask Mr. Ferrell to rewrite the ending. Surely he'd consider it? I mean, how appropriate was it to have two students kiss onstage in front of the entire school, anyway?

I flopped back on my bed with a sigh. And how unprofessional would it be to change the play just because I couldn't stand the lead actor? No, the kiss was going to happen, whether I liked it or not. But I'd just do my best to hold off on it during practice until the last possible minute. Maybe I could fake a late-spring cold or claim that I wanted to have the element of genuine surprise by not rehearsing it.

Jason wouldn't care anyway—with how "boring" and lame as he thought I was, he'd probably be grateful I didn't subject him to it more than once.

My phone buzzed and I grabbed it, expecting a text from Olivia or Lauretta.

Practice tmrw after school in theater? ~ J

The pulse in my throat fluttered wildly. *Jason.*

He hadn't waited for me to send him a text, contrary to his puffed-up declaration in our meeting earlier today. But how did he get my number? He had to have asked one of my friends for it . . . but who gave it to him?

It took me several times correcting the typos caused by my shaky thumb before I managed to reply with, *Yes, see you there.*

With that, I took the script back up and flipped to page one.

Now that our practices were kicking into high gear, it was time for me to work on memorizing these lines.

"Good day, milord," I said in my best British accent as I read the play's opening lines, giving a deep curtsy and using my free hand to hold out my imaginary gown. "May we talk?"

Chapter ● Four

So, how was your play meeting yesterday?" Olivia asked me at lunch the next day. She poked her fork at the slab of uninspiring pizza on her tray, giving a big grimace. "By the way, does it seem lately like the lunch ladies have given up? I mean, look at this—barely any cheese or sauce, and the crust is lumpy and overcooked. Where is the pride and joy in a pizza well done?"

I snorted. "Maybe they're just as ready for the school year to end as we are. It can't be fun, making lunches for hundreds of finicky eaters every day."

I picked up my peanut-butter-and-jelly sandwich and took a huge bite, relishing the rich, creamy peanut butter and sweet tang of grape jelly. Classic perfection.

"That's the best thing about making my own lunch," I

continued after swallowing. "Every sandwich is made with love—and massive amounts of peanut butter. Just the way I want it."

"If you'd start making me sandwiches too, I wouldn't be in this pickle," she retorted in a jokingly snotty tone, rolling her eyes at me. "Anyway, I heard it's a good cast. How is the play itself? Are you excited? Did you already get your script—"

I put my sandwich down and held up my hands, laughing. "Whoa, that's a lot of questions. Um, the play looks like it's a lot of fun. I got the script yesterday and already read it through. It's about two brothers who are in a competition for the same girl, someone they've known since childhood. Naturally, romantic capers and flirty dialogue ensue as the guys try to outdo each other on winning her over."

She put her fork down and smiled. "That sounds like a ton of fun. You're going to do great. And the costumes . . . they're going to be gorgeous, I bet. The play department always has a nice production budget."

"Well, we can use the department's costumes, but I actually want to make my own. Hey, speaking of plays, when do we start working on your puppet stuff? Have you figured out what you want to write about yet? I can help. Maybe something about one of the royal families from that time period?"

"Ooh, great idea!" She rubbed her chin. "I don't know a lot about puppet plays from that time period . . . or if they even had any, actually. Let's walk to the library after school. Maybe we'll find something to inspire us."

"Sure, we can—" I paused. "Oh, wait. Crud. I'm rehearsing today. Jason wants to run lines before we do our first group practice." I desperately tried to ignore the nervous pitch of my stomach at the thought of being alone with him for a full hour.

All I could do was hope he would keep it focused on the play and not say something mean-spirited. I wasn't sure I could put up with it today, not after spending much of the evening and night studying and practicing my lines.

Olivia raised an eyebrow at me. "Soooo . . . everything okay on that front? With Jason, I mean?" Besides the one eyebrow, there wasn't anything else on her face to indicate her emotions. I could tell she was trying hard to school her feelings on the subject, and I appreciated her efforts.

I kept my face as equally neutral, though my pulse picked up in response to the fine line we were dancing. "Good, thanks. No big disasters have happened yet, so here's hoping—"

Someone shoved into my back, pushing me against the table and knocking the breath out of my lungs.

"Sorry!" the guy said to me with a laugh then moved away, disappearing within a cluster of other guys. It was one of Jason's meathead friends—the one from the dance last year, in fact. Figured.

I didn't even bother to respond. I was too busy rubbing my sore ribs. Great company Jason kept, hanging out with jerks like that. I huffed out a breath. Maybe I was being a little unfair, lumping him in with everyone else. Still, that small, frustrated part of me couldn't seem to let it go.

Olivia ripped off a piece of pizza and shoved it in her mouth, chewing unenthusiastically.

I chuckled. "Guess hunger won out, huh?"

She shrugged. "Sometimes we have to just get by until we can have what we really want." There was a strange flatness in her eyes as she spoke.

Was she thinking about Jason? I patted her hand, giving a comforting smile. While I didn't approve of her crush—she deserved *so* much better—I could see how the pains of unrequited love could make everything an aching, complicated tangle. And seeing my friend hurt over a guy broke my heart, regardless of who the guy was.

"You'll find the perfect person someday," I told her warmly. "Someone totally worthy of you."

Olivia looked over at me, giving a weak smile. "Thanks. I know you don't like . . . that is, I know we don't always see eye to eye on everything, but I appreciate you trying." She gave me a big hug, which I returned, squeezing her until she gasped. "I can't breathe, Abbey," she said with a wheeze, laughing.

That got the response I'd hoped for—to help her shake off these blues. I polished off my sandwich and stood. "I gotta run," I told her, glancing at the clock on the wall. "Can't be late for geometry. Miss Pawlinski makes us do math problems on the board if we aren't on time."

She grimaced. "That sounds awful. Go, for heaven's sake. And send me a text tonight to let me know how your practice went."

I nodded and saluted. "You got it, Captain."

"William," I said to Jason in a shaky voice, peeking up from the script into his eyes, "your brother has asked to court me. He wishes to take me horseback riding in the morning."

Jason stared back at me, his own eyes growing wide. He didn't even glance at the script. "Henry?" he scoffed, his eyes suddenly narrowing. "What could he possibly want with *you*?"

The words and sentiment so closely echoed his awful ones from last year's homecoming that I got caught up in the moment and jerked my gaze away. "Um, I—"

Focus, Abbey!

I turned my attention back to the script, but the words were foreign, a bunch of black scribbles. "Shoot," I whispered, sliding off the edge of the stage and scouring the page for my lost line.

The practice this afternoon had been like this from the start, with me flaking out more than I cared to admit. I couldn't focus for more than a minute or two, sitting this close to Jason. All I could do was smell his soft, rich, woodsy scent. Hear the musical cadence in his voice with each line he spoke.

Was it getting warm in here? I looped a finger around my neckline and fluttered it a bit, letting the air waft under my shirt.

"What's wrong?" Jason asked. I could hear a hint of frustration in his voice. "You keep flubbing up the lines."

I turned around, my lips pinched tightly. "We just got the script yesterday. Sorry I'm not as skilled at instant memorization as you seem to be." Embarrassment made me lash out at him a bit harsher than I'd intended, but I was getting a little fed up. He was pushing me too hard, making me even more flustered and awkward.

For the past half hour, it had been a constant back-and-forth between us, filled with Jason's seemingly unending commentary directing me on how I should be speaking my lines:

"No, no, that has less inflection there. Like this."

"You're rushing that part. Let's do it again."

"Where is your emotion? Dig deeper!"

I wanted to throttle him. His ego was so massive, I was surprised he even fit in the theater.

"I don't have it memorized. I . . ." He paused, a bit of the ire fading from his face. "Sorry. I'm a bit of a perfectionist."

"Ya think?" I shot back.

He shrugged. "I believe in doing it until it's right. What's wrong with that?"

"Nothing's wrong with it, but there's a reason it's called 'practice.' We learn new things each time we go through it." I swept a hand across my face.

With violin, I was a big believer in first running through the whole piece in its entirety, going back to see what needed work, practicing those spots a few times, then running through it again. It was a strategy that worked well for me, but it was painfully clear Jason didn't work that way. Nor did he ever want to.

Stubborn and bossy guy.

"This constant rerunning of the same parts, over and over again, has me feeling like I'm spinning my wheels," I continued, biting my lip. "We're not making any forward progress."

Jason hopped down too, looking at me in an unusually open way. "Do you want to take a small break?"

I nodded, plopping down in one of the front-row seats and grabbing my bottled water. My throat was tight, dry, sore, and growing more so by the minute.

Jason studied me in silence as I drank, without any trace of hostility or irritation on his face. The frank appraisal made my throat grow even tighter. What was he thinking? Why was he looking at me like that?

"What?" I blurted out, shaking the water bottle with the force of my question.

A little bit sloshed out the top and sprinkled cold dots onto my jeans. I scrubbed a hand over my thighs, trying to dry them. *Nice job.* The guy was rattling me far too easily. Where was my control?

"You're not what I thought you were," he said quietly.

I wasn't sure how to respond to that. Of course I wasn't. He'd made a hasty assumption about me last year, one that wasn't true. I wasn't boring, contrary to what he and his jerky acquaintances may have thought. I had friends. I had fun. I was artistic and quirky and smart.

I gave a short nod.

He tilted his head, leaning his backside against the stage and crossing his arms. "Why did you audition for the lead, Abbey?"

I blinked. Not a question I'd expected. I put my bottle down, got out of my seat, and drew up to stand on the stage and look around me. The theater was totally quiet—the only sounds were our soft breaths and a few shuffles outside in the hallway. Plush, lightly worn purple velvet seats stared back at me. Thick black curtains framed the stage. Golden, scratched wood flooring rested beneath my feet.

A place where I always ached to belong, with people who would help me find a way to shine.

"Because I wanted to be a part of something amazing," I finally admitted to Jason, surprised at my frankness. I kept my gaze trained away from him, not wanting to see his face right now. Not when I was being so honest. "Music is important to me, and I love playing violin, but there's something about . . ." I flushed, knowing it was going to sound goofy, but I said it anyway. "There's something amazing about *you* being the instrument and bringing the play alive."

Jason hopped up on the stage and stood beside me, casting his gaze out into the theater as well. "I know exactly what you mean." There was a wistful edge in his voice that intrigued me.

Who was he, really? Was he just the shallow guy from the dance last year, or was there more to him? There was a lot I didn't know about this guy, a possible depth to him I never would have guessed.

Perhaps he was a lot different one on one than in a group. More intense.

More . . . real.

I looked over at him. The seating lights played across his face, highlighting the line of his nose, the strong angles of his jaw, the surprising thickness of his lashes. "And why did you audition?" I tossed back at him.

He shrugged. "Lots of reasons. Seemed like fun. A good way to ensure I'd do something I wanted in the Renaissance faire, instead of being assigned to a job I'd probably hate." He paused. "My dad was a theater minor in college. Since I was little, he told me stories about the fun plays and musicals he participated in. I wanted to be a part of something like that too."

"Jason, are we having a moment here?" I asked.

He glanced at me, a small smile on his face. "It would seem so. But don't worry—I'm sure we won't make a habit of it."

I returned the smile, half rolling my eyes. But the tension in my shoulders, my stomach, eased up. Maybe I could get through this without flubbing up anymore. "We should finish up this scene and head out soon. Unfortunately, I have a lot of homework to do. And a play to memorize."

Jason grabbed our scripts and handed mine to me. "Let's take it from the top, shall we?"

Chapter Five

"The muscular system is one of the most vital in the human body. It's the whole reason you're able to move." Mr. Smith jumped out of his seat, the top of his thinning hair fluttering as he practically ran over to the chalkboard. He began scrawling down a bunch of key terms: "bone," "tendon," "epimysium," "perimysium"— and the list kept going. "Muscles work by expanding and contracting . . ."

I'd never seen anyone so excited about muscles, other than the meatheads in the gym who did nothing but pump iron and chug protein drinks.

My hand was cramping from writing down the terms, even though I was only half paying attention to Mr. Smith. The other half of my brain was distracted, which I had been all day.

It started in gym class this morning. Lauretta and I had been talking and walking our laps, as we usually did, when Jason blew by and threw me a challenging look over his shoulder. One I couldn't let go.

With a grin, I took off after him, even as my brain was yelling at me that this was a bad idea—why was I engaging Jason in anything, given how much I couldn't stand him?

". . . bundles of muscle fibers known as fasciles," Mr. Smith droned, interrupting my thoughts.

I glanced at my horrendous spelling of "fascicle" and fixed it then zoned back out again. Jason and I had once again run as hard as we could, this time tying for the lead. It was invigorating . . . until he'd gotten back to his friends and they'd harassed him for several minutes for tying with me.

Put a bit of a damper on the whole thing when I heard him assure them he'd take the lead back tomorrow, because after all, he was in far better shape, being on the baseball *and* golf teams.

My cheeks still burned thinking about it. I could either run full tilt against him and defend myself against his unspoken declaration of my laziness, or I could abstain and face ridicule for chickening out. A lose-lose. And a harsh reminder that he was nothing more than an egotistical jerk.

Somehow, in the intimacy of our rehearsal yesterday, I'd forgotten that simple, straightforward fact. But no more.

Lauretta, who was sitting in front of me, dropped her arm

and reached her hand back to me as subtly as possible. A piece of paper was folded in her fingers.

I dropped my pencil and as I bent to pick it up, grabbed the note, tucking it under my notebook until Mr. Smith went back to drawing and labeling a model of the typical muscle on the chalkboard.

I unfolded the note.

You okay? Seem quiet. Gym still bugging you?

Biting back a sigh, I replied, *I don't know why I let him get to me. It's not a big mystery what a jerk he is. <u>I can't stand him.</u>* I underlined that last sentence just to get the point across.

I passed the note back to her, shaking my head. After the frank conversation during yesterday's private rehearsal, things had gone well. Scarily well, in fact. Jason had backed off being such a control freak, and we'd actually gotten further in the script than I thought we would.

I was an idiot to let my guard down. Something I'd have to remember in future rehearsals. If I was going to be an actress, I had to work at better guarding my true feelings from everyone else, including him. Leaving any room for vulnerability, a way to get hurt again, was not an option.

Lauretta slid back her reply. I opened it.

For someone who dislikes him so much, you spend an awful lot of time talking about him. . . . ;-)

My cheeks flamed up instantly. What was she trying to say, that I actually might not hate Jason? Utterly ridiculous. Besides,

I didn't talk about him that much or hardly think about him at all.

Right?

The bell was going to ring in a couple of minutes, so I crammed the note in my pocket and poked my pencil eraser in her back. I heard her light chuckle float back to me. Lauretta knew how to get me riled up by teasing me, but she wouldn't tell a soul about any of this.

Not that there was anything to tell, of course.

The bell rang. I grabbed my books and got behind Lauretta as we left the room. "What did you mean by that last note?" I asked her.

She waited until we got out in the hallway then tugged me to the side by my elbow. "We've been friends for . . . what, almost five years now?"

I nodded. I'd met Lauretta the first day of middle school. We'd gone to different elementary schools, but the first time we sat beside each other in sixth grade, I instantly knew we were going to be friends. She had a frank, earnest way about her but a warm sincerity that made you want to tell her everything on your heart.

"In all this time I've known you, I've never seen you talk about a guy as much as you do him." Lauretta looked at me, her face completely serious. "I think you need to examine how you really feel about him. The opposite of love isn't hate—it's indifference. If you really didn't care about him, he wouldn't be on your radar at all. The fact that he's able to hurt your feelings so easily is a clear indicator of that to me."

Her words, though quiet, still hit their mark. My chest nearly stung as I soaked in her meaning.

Then, to my horror, my eyes started to burn. Could she be right? Was there a chance that I might actually not hate Jason? That his barbs and gibes at me didn't just make me angry . . . but also hurt my feelings?

"I don't want him to hurt me," I whispered, blinking rapidly to stave off any ridiculous tears from slipping out.

Stupid me, I'd actually let myself like him before then. Olivia and I both had had crushes on him, giggling at sleepovers and trying to decide who he might like. Olivia's crush stayed strong, whereas mine died at homecoming.

Or so I'd thought.

"I don't want you to get hurt either." She squeezed my elbow, empathy deep and warm in her dark-brown eyes. "But like my dad always says to me, if you don't give anything a chance, you'll never really live."

I swallowed, giving her a shaky smile. I couldn't give Jason a chance—nor would I have any reason to. After all, he could barely stand my presence, much less have any feelings toward me.

Why was I even entertaining any of this? *Remember what he said*, I told myself. *He thought you were boring. He pretty much called you lazy today. The guy doesn't care about your feelings at all.*

Lauretta must have sensed the shift in me. She shook her

head, her eyes suddenly sparkling. "Oh, hon. You'd better watch yourself. A guy who has the ability to make you feel such strong highs and lows is dangerous."

My stomach turned with a sense of foreboding. I didn't want to hear what she was saying. I wanted to turn away and run down the hall, out of the building. But she was right about the dangers.

I couldn't let Jason have that much control over me and my emotions.

I gave her a short nod. "I gotta head to class."

She hugged me quickly and said, "I'll talk to you later, okay?"

The hallway was pretty much thinned out by the time I made it to World History, heart thudding dully in my chest. Jason was going to be in there. Which personality would I see this time—the arrogant one or the quieter guy who seemed to have more depth than I'd have guessed?

And which was the real him? I just didn't know.

Olivia waved at me as I slipped into the door, just as the bell rang. "Close call," she whispered.

I gave her a crooked grin and slipped my books under my chair, studiously avoiding looking in Jason's direction. *Get it together*, I ordered myself. *You can do this. You're an actress now, and it's the perfect time to hone those skills.*

Mrs. Gregory started talking, and I focused on the words in front of me, slipping into the role of attentive student. My pen scrawled across the papers as I homed in on her words and studied the terms and images on the chalkboard. I totally had this covered. No sweat.

"Okay, guys." Mrs. Gregory put down the chalk and stood in front of her desk. "Now that I finished all of that 'boring lecture' stuff"—she grinned as she did air quotes with her fingers—"it's time to do something more fun. Let's get started on Renaissance faire planning."

Finally, something engaging. I cast a quick glance at Olivia, who looked back at me and winked.

"I want you to break into small groups of two or three," Mrs. Gregory continued. "You're each likely going to be working on different things, but your purpose today is to help each other brainstorm. What supplies are going to be needed for that person's project? Where should that person start, and what steps have to be finished in what order? In essence, you're going to be temporary partners."

Olivia scooted her desk toward mine. "Okay, awesome. I need some help anyway," she said with a laugh. "I've been trying to think of something to write about for my play, but I'm drawing a blank."

"Maybe I can help?" a husky voice said from behind her.

We looked up to see Jason staring down at us, a light smile on his face. But it was accompanied with a strange tension. He twisted a finger around the hem of his shirt as he peered at Olivia, then me.

Was he . . . nervous?

"Have a seat," I blurted out before I realized what I was saying. For a second, I thought about taking the hasty words back, but if I was going to prove that I was indifferent to Jason, then revoking the invitation would simply show I wasn't as unaffected as I wanted to be.

I could rise above this pettiness and be the bigger person. After all, we were going to be working closely together over the next few weeks for the play. This would be great practice for me.

Olivia's face turned bright red, and she scooted her chair to the side. "You can sit here." She indicated with a nod toward the free space between us. "But be aware that I need a lot of help. I'm so lost." This last part was said with a nervous giggle.

I did my best to hide a cringe.

But Jason gave her a grateful smile and slid his chair over, slipping into it easily. He whipped out a piece of paper. "Ready when you are."

I cleared my throat and turned my focus back to Olivia, trying my hardest to pretend like I didn't notice Jason's knee just inches from mine. The heat seemed to pour off him in waves. "Okay, so since you're doing puppets, you should think about writing a play that's funny or silly."

"Like *Punch and Judy*," Jason said.

"Who?" Olivia turned her wide eyes to him.

He grinned, flashing bright-white teeth. "It's a running set of skits from a long time ago featuring a husband—Punch—and his wife—Judy. They spend the whole time making snarky comments and hitting each other."

"And how do you know so much about puppets?" I asked him.

Olivia shot me a quick glare, but Jason merely laughed. "Too much free time on my hands, I guess," he retorted. "Plus, it doesn't help that I'm actually a big nerd. Don't tell anyone."

I found myself chuckling in response. "I doubt your nerdiness could beat mine. I'm off the charts."

"So," Olivia interjected, turning all of her attention to Jason. "Do you have any suggestions, then? This *Punch and Judy* thing could work, but I wonder if they need to be so mad . . . what if it's less violent and more silly? Like how couples in love tease each other all the time. What do you think?"

It was all I could do to not roll my eyes at her heavy-handedness. Could she be any more obvious in her flirting?

But Jason seemed to eat up the attention. He rubbed his chin, staring at the ceiling as he thought. "I have an idea. What if you do some kind of a spoof off of our play, *All's Fair in Love*? It could be a nice tie-in and get the audience excited to see our performance too . . . and they can figure out all the funny ways you spoofed us when they see your show and then ours."

"That's brilliant!" Olivia said, writing it down.

I hated to admit it, but she was right. Doing a tie-in was quite clever, and our teachers would love that. "You can see my script if you want, so that we can start working on your play." I paused, shooting a look at Jason. "Or better yet, take his. He probably has all of his lines memorized by now, plus mine."

He gave me a casual shrug, but his eyes sparkled. "Guess you'd better catch up or else they'll cast me as a one-man show." He dropped his voice, maintaining eye contact with me. "I can't say I'd look as good as you in a dress, though."

My heart stopped, then restarted again with a furious pace. Jason just complimented me . . . I think. "Maybe it's just a matter of finding the right color and fabric for you," I managed to say. "Have you tried subtle patterns?"

He laughed. "I doubt there's any fabric that can hide these hips," he said, glancing down with a fake woeful expression.

Olivia gave him a fake slug on the arm. The gesture was casual, but her eyes had a strange glint to them as she kept her attention on Jason. "Hilarious!" she said a little too loudly. "Um, so let's get back to the play."

I turned my attention back to my paper and stayed quiet while she and Jason hashed out a few ideas. It was obvious Olivia's flame for Jason hadn't died down . . . and that for some reason, she was determined to make me feel like a third wheel.

Not that I cared, of course. I didn't want to be any wheel, so they could have their special moment together. Didn't matter to me in the least. I spent the rest of class nodding and interjecting when Olivia purposefully looked at me, but otherwise I quietly watched them. They made a great couple . . . if you got past his ego and rudeness and her tendency to overflirt. To be honest, I was kind of surprised he wasn't into her the way she was him. I could see him giving her genuine smiles, fully engaged, but there wasn't a real spark there.

Part of me felt bad for Olivia.

But deep down, a secret part of me I was barely ready to admit existed was also kind of glad.

Chapter • Six

zoomed my lens and snapped a few more pictures of the girls' softball team. The weather outside was perfect, sun warm but not overbearing, a fresh breeze flowing nicely. A quick glance at the screen confirmed I'd gotten several decent action shots. Excellent—this should work just fine.

I peeked at my cell to check the time. Play practice was tonight, but I only had a little homework to do before then. I could walk over to the golf course and take a couple of photos of the students, then call it a day. Things were progressing nicely with the pictures; I was e-mailing them to Robert as I finished, and I'd already done the soccer shots yesterday.

As I walked down the sidewalk and crossed the street to the nearby golf course, I whistled a jaunty little tune, enjoying the sunshine on my face and the top of my head. I took a few shots of birds along the way, just for fun. Maybe I could print these out and put them on my wall to remind me of this weather next winter, when we'd have little sunshine and piles of snow.

When I arrived, the golf course had some adults playing, probably people cutting work. I grinned—Don would be out here if he could. He kept trying to get me to play, but my one venture with golf had left me frustrated and missing the ball far more than I hit it. And when I did make contact, it'd ended up in the sand or water. I had no idea what I was doing wrong.

Don had patted my back several times and encouraged me to try again in the future, but it just wasn't the sport for me. To be honest, I didn't see what was so fun about it; to each his own, I guess.

I traversed the paved cart path, passing each well-manicured hole. I could see students just ahead of me scattered in small groups, whacking the balls with distinct *thwacks*. The small white spheres soared through the air, arcing gracefully then coasting to the fairway. I popped the lens back off and snapped various shots, progressing from hole to hole.

When I got to the seventh hole, I focused on the guy who was carefully practicing his swing. His gestures were graceful, each movement precise. He stepped up to the teed ball, swung the club, and the ball soared forward with a strong hit that made me blink in surprise.

I zoomed in, quickly realizing I recognized that dark, careless hair. And the accompanying self-satisfied grin that went along with an amazing hit.

Jason, of course. Was there anything the guy wasn't talented at?

One of the other guys on the golf team came up and high-fived Jason. "Well done, man!"

Jason shrugged. "Thanks. I've been practicing." He walked over and dropped the club back into his bag. "Good luck."

The guy lined his ball up, took a few practice swings, then whiffed when he tried to hit the ball. I could see the frustration in the stiffness of his back. I waited for Jason to start laughing at him, but he didn't. Instead, he grabbed one of his clubs and went up to the guy's side.

"I think I see what happened here," Jason said. "When you start your swing, your knees are bent perfectly, the way they should be. But when you move the swing forward, you end up standing straight up, so the head of your club is going overtop of the ball. Like this." He demonstrated a couple of times how the guy was doing it wrong.

I moved my camera out of the way, watching carefully. I'd had that same problem when golfing with Don but couldn't figure out why I wasn't connecting with the ball. Maybe my knees were unbending that way when I swung too. Funny how I hadn't even noticed.

The guy nodded. "Okay, I think I get what you mean." He stared down at the ball, bending his knees properly, then swung and kept his legs bent, using his torso to twist and keeping his eyes on the ball. The ball flew down the fairway with ease, lifted on a cushion of air.

"Awesome!" Jason said, beaming. He clapped the guy on the back. "Way to give me a run for my money. You did great that time. Nice job. Keep that up, and you'll be well under par before you know it."

I stared at the scene in confusion, the camera dropping to dangle from the strap around my neck. Who was this version of Jason, so encouraging and . . . nice? I'd never seen him like that before. Yet another layer that made him even more baffling to me.

For the next twenty minutes, I lagged behind the group, taking the occasional shot but keeping the bulk of my attention on Jason. I couldn't help it—as much as I told myself I wanted to ignore him, he was almost magnetic, moving from guy to guy, offering tips and encouraging them. And when he played, his movements were smooth and calm, even if the ball didn't always go where he wanted it to.

So unlike the controlling actor from our play practice, drilling and pushing me to get everything right.

Or the snooty jerk from the dance last year.

I lifted the camera and zoomed to take another shot when Jason suddenly turned toward me, eyes widening as he realized who I was. I dropped the camera in surprise, my neck burning from the rapid rubbing of the strap.

Club in hand, Jason strode toward me, his face now

unreadable. My heart slammed in my chest, even though I wasn't doing anything wrong or creepy. But I felt a bit like a stalker. *No, you're not—you're supposed to be here.*

Still, it took every ounce of self-control I had to stand there and not run off in a guilty dash.

"Hey," he said, eyeing my camera. "What's going on?"

I swallowed, straightening my spine. "Robert asked me to take pictures for the newspaper of some of the sports teams. So I'm here." I lifted the camera. "Uh, taking pictures, of course. With my camera." My cheeks burned as he kept his eyes locked on mine.

When did I become so awkward?

He gave me that toothy grin. "I kind of assumed it was something school-related. Unless you wanted to decorate your locker with pictures of me."

I rolled my eyes, chuckling. "You wish."

"Jason!" one of the guys hollered, waving at him. "We're heading over to the green now."

"I'll catch up in a minute," he replied, then turned back to me. "Do you play golf?"

Part of me wanted to lie and say of course, that I was *amazing,* but if he challenged me to show him my skills, I'd be totally busted.

"My stepdad tried to teach me last fall," I finally admitted, "but I wasn't very good. I kept missing the ball and getting frustrated."

He nodded. "It took me a long time to get used to the different clubs. I'm still working on improving my skills."

Slowly I relaxed. It was so much easier talking to him when he wasn't being overbearing. "Looks like you're doing fine, from what I saw."

He shrugged, giving me a wide grin, not a bit of ego on his face. "I have a long way to go."

This unusual surge of humility was throwing me off-balance. Was he really like this, and the bravado was an act? Or was he just trying to look nicer than he actually was for whatever weird reason?

"Well, I'd better get going," he said, and, if I didn't know better, I'd have sworn I heard a tinge of regret in his voice. "But feel free to follow me around if you want pictures to decorate your house, too."

I barked out a surprised laugh, even as my cheeks blazed with the thought of having his image everywhere. I could tell that this was him teasing and not being an egomaniac; there was that twinkle in his eyes I'd seen in World History class earlier today. "I know your massive self-confidence probably can't believe it, but these pictures aren't for me," I said, giving an exaggerated roll of my eyes. "Besides, I'm sure you have enough girls swooning over you. You hardly need another to add to the list."

"Touché," he replied, his grin growing wider. "But one can never have too many friends, right?"

Were we friends? For so long I'd been angry with him, holding on to a memory that festered in my gut and grew to have a life of its own. But over these last few days, I'd seen more facets to Jason than I'd realized existed. That anger was losing its sharp edge every day.

Maybe I wasn't ready to be friends with him . . . not yet. But acquaintances? I could handle that.

I lifted the camera up and snapped a quick close-up of his face. "That one is for your fan club," I said drolly. "And you'd better go before your team thinks you fell in the water hazard."

He gave me a quick salute. "See you at play practice tonight, Abbey." With that, he walked away, sure and confident.

I tore my gaze away from his retreating figure, popped the lid back on my camera lens, and headed back to the entrance of the golf course, fighting the urge to peek at that impulsive shot I'd taken of his face.

I was late.

I swallowed hard and ran down the dimly lit school hallway, tennis shoes slapping against the floor tiles. My mom wouldn't let me go to play rehearsal until I'd finished all of my chores, and my dawdling at the golf course while taking yearbook pictures had put me behind schedule.

I hoped Mr. Ferrell wasn't going to be mad at me. At least I'd be here, even if it was fifteen minutes late. This was only our second group rehearsal, and I was still anxious to impress him with my professionalism. Being tardy to practice wasn't going to help with that.

I banged through the double doors, rushing down the center aisle. My mouth flew open to exclaim my apologies to anyone who was around, but the words got stuck in my throat. I stopped in place when I realized Jason was on the stage, standing across from Liana. She sidled next to him, eyes intensely locked on his as she replied to whatever he'd said.

Saying my lines.

Whoa, *Liana* was my understudy? How did I not realize this before?

For some reason, the realization unnerved me more than it should have.

A hand tugged my sleeve. It was Mr. Ferrell, coming up behind me. "Let them finish this scene," he whispered under his breath. "Then you can hop up and take Liana's place to start the next scene."

"I'm so sorry I'm late," I whispered back. "I promise it won't happen again." Yeah, I could feed him with a bunch of excuses but in the end, what mattered was I had a commitment and I hadn't followed through on it. Owning up to my mistake was the best thing I could do right now.

He gave a curt nod. "See that you're here on time from now on, okay?" With that, he made his way to the edge of the stage, the script curled in his hand as he followed along with the lines.

I stayed in place, script clutched in my hand, watching

Jason block and recite his lines. He had a good chunk of them memorized, sparing a glance or two at his script every little bit. Bet he had a photographic memory—that would be handy. He moved across the stage, talking, connecting eyes with the other actors as he spoke.

The transformation in his persona was astonishing. I hadn't noticed it in our practice because I was so busy being irritated at his bossiness. But he seemed to be the very embodiment of his role, from the way he spoke to the way he walked. Regal. Proud. Compelling.

Even Liana looked impressed, appreciation lighting up her eyes as she took him in. A swell of jealousy slipped in before I could stop it. What did I have to be jealous about? It had to be because she was in my place right now.

Liana sidled her way up to Jason, draping a hand across his shoulder and leaning in as close as she could, her mouth practically touching his cheek. "Are you jealous of your own brother, sir?"

Jason arched one eyebrow, his gaze raking her face. "Jealous? Me?" His eyes then took on a striking vulnerability, like he was struggling to hide his feelings. He stepped away from her and moved toward the front of the stage, emotion radiating from him.

His gaze connected with mine, and for the briefest moment he paused, looked right at me.

My heart stopped.

"Is it possible?" he murmured, eyes locked on me. "Could I have feelings for her and not have realized it?"

I bit my lip, frozen in place, unable to tear my glance away. I had never been so stripped apart by a mere look in my life. It was almost as if he was speaking to me. About me. The honesty was overwhelming.

"Wonderful job!" Mr. Ferrell said in a loud voice, clapping heartily. His proclamation broke the spell.

Jason blinked and looked over at our teacher, giving him that trademark blinding smile. "Thanks." All traces of the vulnerability I'd seen earlier were swept away, as if they'd never been there. He was himself once again.

I bit my lip harder, jerking myself out of this trance. Ridiculous. What made me think he was talking to me? He was acting. If I were alone, I'd have smacked my own forehead for that gaffe.

Mr. Ferrell jumped onstage and gave Liana a nod. "You did wonderfully. Thanks for filling in." He glanced at me. "Okay, Abbey. We're going to get started on the next scene. Hop on up here. And did you notice the great chemistry between Jason and Liana? She did a wonderful job showing her emotions and confusion about her feelings. Make sure you do the same. We need that to ring true."

I ground my jaw, doubly cursing myself for being late. Not only had I made myself look bad, I'd set myself up to get my acting critiqued and compared to my understudy. I gave him a short nod, trying to shake off my turbulent emotions. "Sure, Mr. Ferrell."

Slip into character, I told myself. I could do this.

Swallowing, I unfolded the clenched script in my fist and wiped my sweaty palm on my pants. All this stuff with Jason was throwing me off-center, and I didn't like it.

Not one bit.

Chapter ● Seven

Jason's basement was nothing like I'd expected.

I followed him through the side door of the brick bungalow and down the dark-brown carpeted stairs, still a little surprised I was even here. The theater was being used by another group today, so we weren't able to do our after-school practice there. Jason had suggested we practice at his house instead.

My first instinct was to say no. It was easier to keep my cool and stay disconnected when I only saw him at school—how would it be if I saw him in such a personal, intimate environment? I was already learning and experiencing things about him I wasn't sure I wanted to know, things that made him a lot more sympathetic than I'd been ready to acknowledge.

But he'd made a good case, arguing that we needed to

maintain our regular rehearsal schedule. I'd reluctantly agreed and after sending Mom a text, we'd walked the short trip to his house.

"Watch your head," Jason said, ducking a little to enter the basement.

I followed his instructions, trying not to notice the surprising wideness of his shoulders as he walked in front of me.

The room was very feminine, with pale pinks and greens accenting the white-shaded palette of the furniture and carpet. There was a TV tucked in a corner, with a couple of video game systems stored nearby. For some reason I'd expected it to be more masculine.

"We can work over here," he said, waving toward the empty corner adjacent to the TV. "My brother will be home soon, but I'll make sure he stays upstairs."

I nodded, dropped my bag onto the couch, and dug out my script. "I think we last left off at the beginning of Act Two." Grabbing the ponytail holder off my wrist, I wrapped my hair into a quick, messy bun.

"I'm not gonna pull your hair, you know," Jason said from behind me, his voice full of mirth.

I turned around, giving him a tight smile. My mind warred with both wanting to push him away and wanting to laugh, connect with him. "Hardy har. It was getting on my nerves, so I pulled it up."

He stepped closer, peering at my locks, then staring into my eyes. He opened his mouth to speak but was interrupted by a loud door slamming.

"Jason!" a small voice called from upstairs. "Where are you? Did you make us peanut butter and apples?"

He cleared his throat. "Um, that's my brother. I'll be right back."

"Jaaaaaaaason!" Little feet trampled the floor right above our heads, resonating through the basement. "I'm so hungry!"

I raised one eyebrow, crossing my arms over my chest and clucking my tongue. "I can't believe you didn't get that boy's snack ready for him. Terrible."

He smirked. "Give me just a moment." Then he darted up the stairs. "I'm right here," I heard him say to his brother. "Did you have a good day at school?"

There was a strange softness in his voice that gave me pause. I stood in place, quiet, just listening.

"It was awesome!" the boy said. "Our teacher said we're going to the zoo next week, and I made a picture for the fridge."

"That's cool, Braedon," he said. There were sounds of doors and drawers opening and closing. "Okay, you have to eat up here. I have a friend over downstairs, and we're practicing for the play."

My throat closed just a little bit. Suddenly I felt embarrassed for eavesdropping and turned my attention toward reading over Act Two.

"Is it a girl?" Braedon asked. "Cuz I thought I heard a girl's voice before."

There was definite laughter in Jason's tone when he replied, "Yes, it's a girl. Now, stay here and eat your apples."

Heavy steps came back down the stairs. I kept my focus on the play.

"Sorry about that," he said. "Um, I'm ready when you are."

"How old is he?" I blurted out, surprising myself. I wasn't trying to pry into his life, but I couldn't help my curiosity.

"Braedon? He's five. Finishing kindergarten this year. He's really smart," Jason said, pride warming his voice. "Do you have any brothers or sisters?"

I dropped the pretense of looking at the play and gazed up at him. "I have an older sister, Caroline. She's a senior at our school—two years older than me."

He tilted his head, appearing deep in thought. "Oh wait, I know who you're talking about." His brow furrowed slightly as he stared at me. "Wow, I didn't know *she* was your sister."

Caroline and I looked nothing alike. She had lush blond hair and slender curves, whereas I was short and had dishwater-blond hair. But for some reason, hearing him say it, reminding me how pretty my sister was compared to me, soured my light mood. "Yeah, I know. I hear that a lot. Anyway, we need to practice. I gotta get home and do homework soon."

He blinked then recovered, his tone taking a bit of a cool edge. "Yeah, sure, whatever."

We ran through lines for a good twenty minutes, awkward tension building between us. My lines fell flat, the usual jovial, teasing tone not there. Fortunately for me, Jason's performance wasn't that much better. He seemed distracted, stopping and starting in strange bursts.

Did I throw him off because of my mood change? I couldn't read him right now. What was he thinking?

A torrent of small footsteps flew down the stairs. "Jason!" Braedon said. "I'm bored. I wanna play a video game."

He huffed a sigh. "Not right now."

Braedon planted his hands on his hips, a stubborn set to his jaw. His dark hair was ruffled wildly, and in that moment I could see a clear resemblance between them, both in personality and looks. "Mom already said I could." His tone dared Jason to refute that proclamation.

I smothered a laugh behind my hand. "He's got you there," I said.

Jason eyed me, a slow smile crawling on his face. The crackling tension between us disappeared. "You *would* take his side."

"He's obviously the cute one in the family," I said with a casual shrug.

"Milady, you wound me," Jason teased with mock hurt, clapping a hand over his chest.

"What are you two talking about?" Braedon asked, eyeing Jason then me.

I straightened the smile on my lips and looked at him. "I'm teasing your brother because he likes to think every girl loves him." A glance at Jason showed me a surprise—two bright blooms of color on his cheeks.

Did I embarrass him?

Braedon apparently got bored with the conversation, because he ran over to the video games and started putting one in. The TV cranked on, booming in the room.

Jason sighed, his hand dropping to his side and the script fluttering from the movement. "It's apparent we're not going to get anything more done today," he said, clearly exasperated.

"Eh, I need to run anyway." I gathered up my stuff and slung my bag over my shoulder.

"We'll pick somewhere else to rehearse next time," he said, following me up the stairs and to the side door. "Our neighbor has offered to watch Braedon on days I practice at school, so that won't be a problem."

I paused and turned around. "Um, thanks. For having me over, I mean." Now I was the one with the blush; I could feel it warming my cheeks.

Jason paused in the doorway and peered down at me. His eyes were intense, taking me in. Something silent and unspoken crackled between us in that moment. It scared me. It invited me closer.

"Do you want me to walk you home?" he asked, his voice husky.

No. Yes. I shook my head slightly. "I'm . . . okay, thanks. You should stay here and watch your brother. He seems like a handful."

He gave me a crooked grin, his eyes warm and open and staring at me so intently, I found myself staring right back.

How many other people has he practiced this smile on? some part of my brain whispered.

That did the job. I cleared my throat and backed away. "I gotta go. Bye." With that, I turned and took off down the sidewalk, refusing to look back. I didn't want to be a practice dummy for his flirtation skills. I deserved better than that.

And it couldn't possibly be true that any of that emotion he'd shown me was genuine.

Not at all.

"I haaaaate math," Olivia whispered to me. Her utter misery was etched on her face. "I thought geometry was going to be easier than algebra. But it's just as awful, and I hate it just as much."

Luckily, we were in the back row of the room, so our teacher couldn't hear us talking.

"It's not so bad," I whispered back. Heck, I could take math any day of the week. What was *really* hard was struggling with my ever-conflicting feelings about Jason. Last night I'd lain in bed for a long time, thinking about his eyes.

His eyes! How ludicrous was that? I could kick myself for being so ridiculous about him.

I was getting caught up in the romantic nature of the play, letting it sweep me away. I couldn't forget how he really was, *who* he really was. But I was perilously close to overlooking more and more of that reality every time I was around him.

Mrs. Washburn sat behind her desk, droning on about

whatever our lesson was today. I was too distracted to pay much attention. I'd noticed that Jason wasn't in gym class today. Instead of enjoying the reprieve with Lauretta, I'd spent the whole time wondering why he was absent. Was he sick? Injured? Would he still be coming to play practice tonight?

Of course, I'd tried to convince myself my caring was only because he was the male lead, and given how badly our practice yesterday afternoon in his basement went, we needed all the time we could get.

But my gut knew that he was getting stuck in my thoughts more and more every day, and that it had nothing to do with the play.

"Wanna do homework after school today?" Olivia asked me.

I gave her an absent nod.

"What's with you? You seem . . . distracted."

Biting back a sigh, I said, "Um, just have a lot on my mind."

"Such as . . . ?"

"I'm just—I'm worried about how the play practice is going. It doesn't seem to be progressing the way I'd want it to." There, that was nice and generic. Hopefully we could avoid talking about—

"Jason seems to be very focused," she said, her voice turning even breathier than usual. "I've seen him running his lines at lunch a couple of times. And some of the other girls in the play say that he's doing a great job."

Irritation welled in me, making me sound snottier than I intended. "Yeah, sure looks like he is."

Either Olivia didn't notice my tone or she didn't care. Her fingers ripped tiny shreds in the corner of her notebook page as she stared at her notes. "I wish I'd tried out for the play. Then I could be near him and get to know him better. You're so lucky."

"I don't feel lucky," I muttered darkly.

Her back stiffened. "Why not? You have an important role in the play. You are a featured person, a star. I'm going to be stuck either handing out hunks of meat or hiding behind a curtain playing with puppets."

A wave of humility washed through me. "I'm sorry," I said, meaning it. "I don't mean to take it for granted. You're right. I'm lucky to have gotten where I am." All this nonsense with Jason was making me lose focus of my goals and what mattered: using this chance to gain real credentials in the arts.

The bell rang, dismissing us for the next class. We gathered up our stuff, waiting for the crush of students to disperse before going to the doors.

Her tone turned tentative as she turned to me. "I know you don't like Jason, and I know we're not supposed to talk about it, but I feel like you're being really unfair. I'm holding back my thoughts on it so it won't cause problems, but it's getting harder to do when you gripe so much."

Now my back stiffened. Yeah, I'd fussed about him a few times, but I wasn't griping *that* much. Was I? "You may be able to let things go faster than me, but that doesn't make my feelings wrong."

She blew out a frustrated breath. "I didn't say your feelings were wrong. But I think you're being too judgmental. You need to let it go. He's not a bad guy."

"No, he's not." I remembered the way he'd laughed with his brother yesterday, their easy camaraderie. I shoved the books closer to my chest, wishing I could hold on to my spite. Wishing things weren't changing so fast.

Olivia turned her head, studying my face for a moment, unblinking. "What's the real reason you're so upset with him?" she suddenly asked.

I knew what she was really prodding me about. She wanted to know if deep down I had any feelings for him. But what could I tell her? *Yes, I do, but I don't trust him enough to let myself fully feel them because he'll only hurt me again if I do? And just as bad, I don't trust you enough to admit those feelings to you?*

So I scoffed instead, shoving back the words I really wanted to say. "You know why I'm feeling like this. It's because I see him every day, acting superior to everyone else."

Even as I said it, I knew the words weren't fully accurate. Jason hadn't acted superior on the golf course the other day when helping other students practice their swings, but I couldn't tell Olivia the truth.

Because if she knew I was starting to soften toward him, then our tentative truce on Jason would be broken. I'd be her competition for his affections, even if I didn't intend to be. It might drive a wedge between us permanently.

She stared hard at me for another long moment. I couldn't tell if she believed me or not, if she felt any of the conflicting emotions I was sure radiated off me like the sun. Her lips were pinched, her eyes disappointed. "I don't know what else to say about this," she finally said. "I'll talk to you later." Then she walked up the aisle and left the room.

I followed behind her, both relieved and frustrated that I'd escaped her scrutiny for now.

Things were getting far too complicated.

Chapter Eight

My violin sang in the theater.

From my chair on the stage, I slipped the bow across the strings, eyes glancing over the sheet music. I'd played this piece enough now that I practically knew it by heart, but better to be safe than sorry. It was an upbeat song, with lots of staccato sixteenth notes. My toe tapped merrily along.

Each note resonated in the theater, punctuating the silence. It was a concert for one, playing music for myself.

My fingers flew across the strings as I neared the frantic, emotional ending of the piece. The music swelled, crested, reaching the top rafters as I let myself play the way I always wanted to—boldly, without fear.

I swiped my bow for the final note then stopped, letting the moment sink deeply into me.

A small clap came from the back corner.

Startled, I nearly dropped my violin. I turned away from the music stand and stood to stare into the seats. I'd turned on only the stage lights, not bothering to illuminate the rest of the large room.

Who was here?

Our play rehearsal wasn't starting for another twenty minutes. I'd forgotten my violin in my locker today in my rush to get home, so I came back to school early to squeeze in a little practice time. No one was supposed to be around. I could train to my heart's content.

Jason swept forward from the dark corner of the farthest wall, padding down the side aisle and hopping onstage. His face was animated in a way I'd never seen before, eyes alight with interest. "That was amazing," he said. "I had no idea you could play like that. How long have you been playing violin?"

There was genuine excitement in his words, enough that I found myself warming up to him in return. I put the violin and bow on my chair. "I started in fourth grade and fell in love with it."

"I play music too," he said. "Bass guitar." There was a slight edge of hesitation in his voice as he spoke, and if I hadn't grown attuned to his speech patterns I probably would have missed it. "But I only started last year." He glanced at my violin then at me, giving a shrug that was far too casual and didn't match the tone of his voice.

Was he nervous?

Something inside me cracked and softened at the realization of his vulnerability right now. I'd seen him arrogant, authoritative, even educational, but not like this. Perhaps music was as important to him as it was to me.

"What made you choose bass?" I asked. The unspoken question was, why not lead guitar, or singer? I would have thought he'd crave the attention that came with being the front man.

He dropped to sit on the edge of the stage and I joined him. I could smell fresh soap on his skin, see the damp curls of hair around his forehead. He'd showered before play practice. "It seemed like fun. I've always enjoyed music but never tried it before. But a friend told me I should give it a chance." He paused, slid a glance over at me. "I still have a long way to go."

This strange show of humility once more was messing with my head. He sounded genuine. "Why were you out of school today?" I asked, then wished I could take the words back. It was far too nosy. It showed I was paying attention to him.

The grin that creased his face, dimpled his cheeks, said he picked up on my concerns. "Why, did you miss me?"

I rolled my eyes. "You wish."

He simply looked at me in response. My heart thudded hard.

Maybe a stupid, strange part of me had missed him. Could he tell? I swallowed, licked my suddenly dry lips.

His gaze glanced to my mouth then back up to my eyes. "We have to kiss," he whispered.

My lungs clenched into two painfully small fists. I pressed my fluttering hands against my thighs, wiping the sudden burst of sweat that broke out on my palms.

Jason wanted to kiss me.

I found my lips parting on their own, unable to stop myself from leaning forward just a little bit.

His eyes were locked on mine, dark and swirling with emotion. He parted his lips as well, moving toward me until he was only a few inches away. His breath came in small, soft puffs on my mouth. "I . . . well, I'd meant in the play . . ."

Idiot! I chastised myself, a painful burst of heat crawling across my cheeks. What was I thinking?

I closed my eyes and backed away, wishing I could sink beneath the stage. Hide until this horrible embarrassment faded away. Which should only take, oh, another fifty years or so. What made me think he meant right now, when there was obviously nothing between us?

And even worse, why had I wanted him to kiss me?

"I knew what you meant." My words stung as I spoke, falling sharper than a razor's edge. I wiped my palms on my thighs again and stood to break down my music stand and pop my violin and bow back into my case. With every ounce of dignity in me, I kept my spine straight and ignored Jason's eyes, which I could feel on my back. No way did I want to look at him and possibly see laughter.

Or even worse, pity.

My hands stayed mostly steady, only shaking once or twice. I could almost be proud of my coolness, if I hadn't let myself get weak in the first place.

"Abbey," he started, a slight hitch in his voice. I heard him stand up, take a step toward me. "Um, I—"

The door flung open, and Mr. Ferrell loudly proclaimed, "Great! Both of my leads are here. I hope you're ready to pack some emotion into today's practice! We have a lot of ground to make up."

Keeping my attention on Mr. Ferrell and not looking at Jason at all, I nodded and gave a huge smile, as genuine as I could muster. "Of course!" I said. "I've been practicing at home. I'm ready."

I hopped off the stage and busied myself with putting my case and music on a nearby seat, still not ready to look at Jason. Willing my face to stop burning. I could have kicked myself for being so stupid.

More of our fellow actors started flitting in, their conversations filling the awkward gaps. I looked attentive as they spoke to me, making myself smile and nod in the right places, though in reality, I barely understood a word.

All I could think about was Jason's soft lips, so close to mine.

A kiss that never happened.

I grabbed my script, put on my best face, and got back onstage, walking to the spot where Mr. Ferrell pointed. It was better this way. I needed to stay focused on what really mattered instead of letting anything distract me.

Somehow, I managed to fake my way through rehearsal. The whole time, my eyes never quite met Jason's, nor did his meet mine. The awkwardness beat at me relentlessly, forcing me to be even more aware of him than usual. Every movement of his body, the cadence of his voice.

It was maddening, but at least Mr. Ferrell didn't seem to pick up on it. I guess we were both doing a great job of acting. Jason, pretending as the male lead that he had genuine feelings for me.

And me, pretending nothing Jason did mattered to my ego or my heart.

The weekend couldn't come soon enough.

I spent much of Saturday puttering around my room. I cleaned my closet and hung my clothes according to color. Rearranged my bookshelves alphabetically, first based on author then on title. My dresser drawers were spotless, every outfit folded neatly and tucked inside.

I even vacuumed and swept and dusted. When my mom had seen me reaching for the dust cloth, she'd blinked in surprise.

All of it was a desperate, futile attempt to shake off anything to do with the play. Since that awkward rehearsal and the not-kiss, I'd been doing anything and everything possible to avoid thinking about Jason. Friday night I'd realized that maybe I just needed a break.

All work and no play, as they said. So I closed my script and turned my attention elsewhere.

At least I had tonight to look forward to. Saturday nights were my hangout times with Olivia. She came over for dinner, endured my stepdad's goofy teasing and asking how many hearts she'd broken that week, then we stayed up way too late in the family room, eating popcorn and snacks and watching a bunch of romantic comedies.

Our weekly ritual. One I especially needed tonight.

There was a knock on my door, then my mom peeked her head in. "Hey, you okay? I've never seen you clean like this before."

I smiled. "It was long overdue." I straightened the papers on my desk as she slipped inside, closing my bedroom door behind her.

"Honey, everything okay?" she asked, perching on the edge of my bed. Worry lines creased her brow.

"Sure, why wouldn't it be?" I nodded hard, but even I could hear the fakeness in my voice, the strain to pretend everything was fine.

She pursed her lips, scrutinizing me for a moment. "Is this about the play practice? Is it too much for you to handle? Because if it is—"

"No, no, that's fine," I blurted out in a rush. If she thought I was having a hard time balancing everything, she'd make me bow out of the play. Then Liana would get the lead, and I would be stuck doing something far less satisfying for the Renaissance faire. "Just . . . having a bit of a rough week, that's all. You know how that goes."

Mom gave me a gentle smile. "Okay. If you need to talk, you

know where to find me." She patted my shoulder and stood. "I'm making spaghetti and meatballs tonight for dinner, by the way."

I gave Mom a genuine grin in thanks. "Olivia's favorite. She'll be thrilled." She and I usually were at each other's houses so often that our parents knew what each other's favorite foods were. Sometimes, Olivia's mom would make barbecue chicken pizza for me. I always ate way too much of it.

"Well, I'd better go back downstairs." With one last sweeping look at me, Mom left and closed my door behind her.

Still wearing a smile, I dropped down on my bed, grabbed my phone off the nightstand, and sent Olivia a text. *Spag and meat-balls for din. Yum! :-)*

My phone buzzed a couple of minutes later. *Can't make dinner, sorry. Too much homework.*

I swallowed, trying to ignore the sinking feeling in my gut. Olivia had never brushed off our Saturday plans to do homework. She either brought it with her or crammed quickly beforehand so she could be free. *Everything okay?* I texted back.

It was another couple of minutes before she responded. *Just busy. Will talk to you later.*

The emotion in my gut roiled, turned to an edge of irritation. That was definitely a brush-off. Great. I didn't even bother to reply, just crammed my cell in my jeans pocket and huffed out an exasperated sigh.

What was her problem, anyway? I didn't do anything to her. Everything had seemed fine after school on Friday, though she was a little quieter than usual. But she'd blamed it on having a headache.

Did this have to do with Jason?

It had to. Nothing else in our lives was causing such conflict as him. I pinched my lips, fighting the urge to call her and demand she tell me what's wrong. Olivia was a horrible liar; I could see right through her text plain as day.

I'd give it until tomorrow and then call to see what's going on. Obviously she needed some time to herself. A swell of hurt feelings made my heart ping. Tonight wouldn't be the same without her.

I shuffled downstairs and made my way to the kitchen. Mom was at the counter, buttering bread and sprinkling garlic salt on it.

"What time will she be here?" she asked.

"She's not coming."

Something in my voice must have alerted her to my volatile feelings because for once, she didn't pry. Instead, she gave me an apologetic smile. "Okay, can you help set the table for me?"

Grateful for a distraction, I did as she asked, grabbing napkins and silverware and glasses.

"Hey, dork," Caroline said, patting me on the shoulder. She took some of the silverware and helped me set the rest of the table.

"Don't set a fifth spot," I said. "Olivia's not coming."

"How come?"

Obviously she wasn't as sensitive to my tone as Mom was. "Because she's busy doing homework tonight."

Caroline raised one blond brow, a perfect look of skepticism on her face. "Homework? On a Saturday?"

My answering shrug was tight.

She skipped over the seat where Olivia would have sat, placing a fork and knife at Don's place. "All righty, then."

Dinner was quiet. I could tell they were trying hard not to press me about Olivia's absence. All I could think about was her shortness in her text.

And about Jason. The more I got to know him, the more complicated he seemed. At times unbearable, and at other times compelling. Why was he messing up my life so much? Why was I giving him that power?

That almost-kiss still haunted me. When we actually did have to kiss for the play . . . what would it be like? Would his mouth be as soft as it seemed? Would he like it?

Would I?

"Stop playing with your food, Abbey," Mom admonished.

I glanced up to see her staring at me.

"You've been pushing that meatball around for five minutes." Her voice got gentler. "How about you clear your plate and give someone a call? Like Lauretta? I bet she'd come over to hang out with you. Or you two could go to the mall or something."

Maybe Mom was right. Lauretta was fun. She wouldn't avoid me because of guy issues.

I cleaned up quickly, eager to push all thoughts of Olivia and Jason from my mind. "Thanks, Mom. I think I will."

Chapter ● Nine

"What happened this weekend?" I whispered to Olivia as we stood in the school parking lot on Monday morning. I'd tried to call her yesterday, but she didn't answer her phone. "You never called me back. Why?"

This was the first time I'd talked to her in two days. We'd never gone that long without talking.

Ever.

Olivia had the grace to bashfully look at me, a tinge of regret in her eyes. "Sorry. I . . . I had some personal turmoil going on." She paused, leaned closer so the other World History students around us wouldn't hear. "I had some thinking to do about this stuff with . . . you know who. Just had some things to sort out in my head, and I wasn't ready to talk to you about it yet."

I knew exactly who she meant. I couldn't help my glance going over to look at Jason, who stood talking with a couple of his guy friends. He had on a navy-blue shirt and jeans that looked like they were made just for him. The breeze ruffled the top of his hair, and he squinted against the early-morning sun.

We were all waiting for the school bus to take us to the Cleveland art museum, our end-of-year field trip for World History, where we would spend time in the medieval section, looking at tapestries, art, and armor. A nice way to kill a school day, and something I'd completely forgotten about (thanks to all this drama with Olivia and Jason) until Mom reminded me this morning.

I sighed. "I don't like that a guy can come between us like this."

"I know." She elbowed me lightly in the side, giving a small half smile. "Yesterday evening I felt dumb about being upset over this, but I didn't know how to call you and tell you. It was stupid for me to react that way. I realize that now. After all, it's not like you like him, right? I mean, we're not competing for him or anything."

With everything in me, I fought the heat threatening to erupt across my face. How could I possibly explain my conflicted emotions about Jason? "No, not at all," I answered passionately, pressing my notebook against my chest.

After all, I didn't like Jason in that way. He made me utterly crazy, and I didn't need more drama in my life right now, other than the school play.

She released a sigh and seemed to relax; her face glowed with her easy smile. "Sorry, I should never have doubted you." She squeezed me quickly then squealed when the bus showed up. "Oh, it's time to go! I'm so excited."

It was hard for me to scrape up much enthusiasm about the trip. I was still awkward with Olivia, and squeezing in next to her on the seat near the back of the bus didn't make anything more comfortable. All it did was make me realize that Olivia was a lot more head over heels for him than I'd originally suspected. I would have to walk on eggshells with her and not bring him up at all.

Frustrating. Disappointing.

Could a guy really come between us? I never would have imagined it, never would have thought our friendship could be so unstable.

Guess I was wrong.

Mrs. Gregory swept up and down the center aisle, counting heads with her mouth moving. "Okay . . . looks like everyone is here." She beamed. "Wonderful! I'm looking forward to this. Now, stay seated, and don't act up." With one final warning glare at the guys, she moved up to the front row and sat down in an aisle seat.

The bus rumbled awake and pulled out of school. Voices chattered around us; Olivia and I stayed quiet for several minutes.

"I'm sorry," she finally said, her voice barely discernable above the roar of the road below us and the crowd around us. "I really am. I should have talked to you instead of shutting you out."

I gave her the best smile I could muster and laid the notebook on my lap. "Okay." I couldn't shake off my uneasy feeling, though.

From my place in the aisle, I scanned the faces around me. My eyes connected with Jason's, who was doing the same from his seat a couple of rows ahead. I swallowed and looked away, pushing back the strange thud in my chest that came when I saw his deep eyes fixed on me.

"So," I said to Olivia, "What do you want to see at the museum today?"

"Hmm." She rubbed her chin. "I love the armor room, of course. But I also like the paintings. All those beautiful colors and smiling women. The rolling fields and grasses." She sighed happily. "It's heaven. What about you?"

"I love the tapestry room. And the artwork, too, like you. And the furniture."

Mom and Don had taken Caroline and me to the art museum a few months ago. I was looking forward to seeing it again and hopefully getting more entrenched in the Renaissance world, living and breathing this era. Being surrounded by its art should work nicely.

And it would definitely help me keep my attention on school and the faire's play, where it belonged.

The bus's wheel dipped into a pothole. In unison, we were all jarred out of our seats. The whole bus cried out in surprise, then laughed as a group. I shifted and resettled myself on the faux-leather bench seat.

I found myself drawn to Jason's face once again. It was in

profile, the strong nose standing proud, teeth white, jaw firm, dimpled cheeks from his laugh. As much as I hated to admit it, he was magnetic. He made a perfect romantic lead.

He threw his head back and laughed at something the person across from him said. I couldn't hear them, but could see the sweeping line of his throat. My own throat grew a little dry, and I swallowed.

I didn't want to be attracted to him.

And yet I was.

In spite of everything, I couldn't deny it anymore. I needed to stop lying to myself.

The bus drove on. We bounced along, people around me talking nonstop. Olivia talked too about nothing important, just flitting from topic to topic. I nodded and murmured in the appropriate places, but there was an odd flutter just beneath my skin. An awareness of Jason I couldn't turn off. It was like I was hypersensitized to him, tuned in to the frequency of his voice.

How could I *like* him? When had it happened?

At some point in all of this mess, I'd stopped thinking of him as a complete jerk and started finding things I didn't hate about him. Things I may even have admired. Or actually found myself drawn to.

His smile. His laugh. The way he helped others. His vulnerability at times. The easy relationship with his brother.

His love of music, equally matched by mine.

But so what if I did like him? It didn't matter anyway. There's no way things between us were going to go anywhere. He didn't like me back, after all. Disappointment roiled in my stomach, and I fought back a sigh, leaning heavily against the seat. Besides, I didn't want Jason to like me. Not at all. That would make things a hundred times more complicated.

At least right now I could keep my feelings to myself. Then once the play was over, it would fade away, and I could go back to feeling normal again.

I hoped.

The bus driver pulled into the front of the art museum. A few students cheered as we slowed to a stop.

Mrs. Gregory stood, sweeping her gaze over all of us. "I expect you all to be on your best behavior," she admonished. "You represent our school. If you act up, you will spend the rest of the trip sitting on the bus. And I *will* be calling your parents."

Some smart-mouthed guy behind me said, "Ooooh," but quietly enough that Mrs. Gregory didn't hear. I turned and shot him a small glare, which he didn't even bother to acknowledge.

We exited the bus and made our way across the slick, clean tile floor and up the massive marble staircase, winding and weaving to the entrance of the armor room. Mrs. Gregory led the way, her plaid skirt swirling around her legs and her sandals flopping as she hustled forward.

She stopped, turned to the whole group. There was an excited smile on her face. "I want you to take your time and really explore this area, you guys. Take notes. Draw pictures. You're being shown a window into a fascinating era. Take advantage of it. You can use this information to supplement both our class and your knowledge of the period itself. It will make your Renaissance faire all the more authentic." She glanced at her watch then back at us. "Okay, meet me back here in an hour, on the dot. Do *not* be late."

A group of guys took off, slowing down when one of the museum guards shot them a glare.

"Where to first?" Olivia asked me.

"Um, how about we just start along the walls and work our way around the room?"

We stepped inside, and the armored horse in the center of the massive room grabbed my attention instantly.

"Look how small the knight is," Olivia said, pointing at the armored man mounted on top of the horse. "For some reason I thought he'd be . . . taller."

I laughed. "I think people were shorter back then." I stared up and at the tops of the walls, which were decorated with colorful woven tapestries and various weapons. "How cool is that?" I said, nodding at the walls. What would it have been like to live in a castle, adorned with those kinds of decorations?

"If you like those, you should see the tapestry room," a deep voice said from just over my shoulder. Soft puffs of his breath caressed my cheek.

I bit my lip to hide my surprise. "I saw it for a minute the last time I was here," I told Jason. "But I'll have to go back in and see it again."

Olivia noticed Jason beside me. Her eyes went from him to me then back to him, opening wider. She smiled. "Let's go check out some of the weapons."

Jason stayed between us as we walked over to the fringes of the room, looking at poles, axes, swords, and rapiers. I kept a smile pasted on my face for so long my cheeks began to hurt. He and Olivia talked about the different weapons; I merely followed along and smiled, trying to not notice the richness of his cologne or the heat coming from his body as his arm brushed against mine.

Every nerve on my skin was on high alert and focused on him. It was maddening, and yet bizarrely intoxicating at the same time. Had I ever been so aware of another person before? I didn't think so.

He laughed at something Olivia said and we kept walking.

"Imagine trying to fight with a helmet like that on," Olivia said, pointing to a strange spiked one. "How difficult would that be?" Her voice was breathy, full flirtation engaged and locked on Jason.

My smile slipped a bit, guilt twinging my stomach. Guilt and irritation. And guilt because of my irritation. Olivia had a right to flirt with him all she wanted. I'd told her I wasn't interested in him. And here he was, talking and flirting right back, showing her all those dimples and neat rows of blazing white teeth. Eyes flashing in response to everything she said.

I was pretty much forgotten by both of them.

My irritation swelled to include him, too, and the rest of my smile slid off my face. I stepped back from them and forced myself to relax. This was getting ridiculous. I needed a moment to collect myself.

"I'll be back in a minute," I mumbled and turned on my heel, fleeing into another room right off the main armor room.

Olivia was too busy laughing at something Jason said to notice my departure. The sound followed me out.

A few students flitted around the room, looking at various paintings with rich colors and lush brushstrokes, women in fluffy gowns and coiled hair. I kept my distance from them, sitting down on a bench to look at a painting of a sunset in a valley. The colors and gentle image soothed me a little bit.

Things were starting to get out of control. If I was this frustrated from Jason and Olivia just having friendly conversation, how much worse was it going to get by the end of the year? How was I going to continue to fake my way through this?

I leaned over, elbows on my knees, and dropped my head in my hands. Why did I have to like him, of all people?

A hand tapped my shoulder. I jerked, looked up to see Jason peering down at me, a deep frown between his eyes.

"You okay?" he asked, concern pouring through his voice.

I couldn't help the warmth that flooded me at the genuine emotion coming off him. "Um, yeah. Sorry, I'm fine." I gave a small, polite smile to mask my feelings. "Where's Olivia?"

"She went to the restroom. Apparently it's a trek downstairs." He slid onto the bench beside me, his muscled thigh not even an inch from mine. All that exercise with baseball and golf sure was working.

I tore my gaze away from his toned physique to stare fixedly back at the art on the wall. *Stop acting stupid*, I ordered myself. Who cared if he smelled amazing? *Don't forget why you didn't like him in the first place.*

It was getting harder to remember the reasons.

"We need to talk," Jason suddenly said, and the quiet force behind his words grabbed my attention.

I looked at him, my heart thudding so hard I was sure he could hear it. "What about?"

He stared back, his eyes intense. "I think you know."

My throat went dry again. I swallowed twice. "No, I don't. What could we possibly have to discuss?"

"Hey!" The exclamation came from a couple of Jason's friends who came into the room, scooting onto the bench beside Jason.

"There you are," a tall guy named Camden said. He glanced over at me then back at Jason. "What are you doing?"

I stood. "Nothing. I need to go."

I got a step away before my hand was captured in a warm, firm grip. Instant heat flooded me. I turned to see Jason looking up at me, his gaze just as firm as his hand.

"We need to talk. After school."

All I could do was nod. I extricated my hand from his grasp and walked back toward the armor room, my fingers tingling.

Chapter ● Ten

It was hard to concentrate on anything meaningful for the rest of the field trip. Our class spent another couple of hours wandering the exhibits, absorbing the artwork. After coming back from the bathroom, Olivia had found me and grabbed my arm, keeping me firmly tucked by her side the rest of the time.

Normally I wouldn't be suspicious of that. After all, she was a friend who always liked to hug and be really close, with no personal boundaries. But now that Jason was a "thing" between us, I couldn't help but wonder if she was keeping me with her so she could track my whereabouts.

After all, if I was at her side, I wasn't at his.

It was ridiculous to think that, and I was embarrassed to be suspicious this way. Embarrassed, but not enough to stop me from worrying about it.

Still, I played along with her and talked, laughed, and smiled as we wove our way through the exhibit rooms. Large pieces of antique furniture, rich paintings, compelling sketches drew our attention quite easily from any uncomfortable topics. We didn't run into Jason at all, and I couldn't help wondering where he was.

And what he wanted to talk about with me.

Did he know about my conflicted feelings for him? Why had he touched my hand earlier to get my attention? I could still feel his fingers wrapped in mine for that brief moment. Warm, firm. Compelling.

Around noon, Mrs. Gregory rounded us back up. We had lunch in one of their art rooms, sandwiches and chips provided courtesy of our school, while a curator discussed the ins and outs of finding, acquiring, and displaying medieval art, armor, and artifacts. The woman spoke drolly, her tone flat and unengaging; it was hard to keep my attention on her and not look behind me to see where Jason was.

But I didn't want Olivia to know I was even thinking about him, much less wanting to see where he sat.

Ugh, this was getting ridiculous.

I finished the last of my sandwich and balled up the wrapper and brown paper bag in my fist.

Mrs. Gregory stood in front of us, leaning against the front wall. "The bus will be here any moment to pick us all back up. When we return to school, you guys will spend the rest of the day in the library, working on researching your projects, costumes, whatever you need to do. I'll be checking in with you individually on Friday to see how you're progressing."

At least we didn't have to go back to class. Several cheers around me confirmed that other students felt the same way. I grinned.

"Can you help me work on my play?" Olivia asked me. She crammed a few chips into her mouth, chewing fast.

I nodded. "I have a copy of the play in my book bag. We can draft your puppet play quickly, I'll bet. It'll be fun." I recalled the teasing lilt to Jason's voice when we'd had our planning meeting last week.

Nope, not thinking about him. I pushed that aside and made my smile even bigger. Fake it till you make it, right?

The bus ride back to school was louder than the ride to the museum. For the most part, I managed to tune out everyone around me. Olivia didn't say much, busying herself with writing notes and sketching in her notebook, so I was able to escape into my own thoughts, carefully maintaining my concentration on my lap, my notebook drawings, anywhere but on him.

Even still, his presence seemed to beckon me.

It felt like ages before the bus pulled into the parking lot. We made our way off the bus and back into school, heading to our lockers to grab supplies and then to the library, where our two elderly librarians waved us inside.

"Our books on the Renaissance era are back here," Miss Wallingham said. Her wiry white hair was pulled into a sharp, crisp bun, and she wore a mauve dress with mauve flats. "Let me or Miss Lasko know if you have any questions. We're happy to assist with research if you need it."

Miss Lasko, who looked nearly identical to Miss Wallingham except for having on a blue dress and black vest, nodded. "We have a lot of great material at your disposal. Make good use of it."

Olivia and I went right for a corner of an empty table, tucked near the back of the library, by the massive windows. We plopped our stuff down and leaned back in the old wooden chairs.

"That was a fun trip," she said, eyes shining. "My mom said she was going to buy me some fabric this weekend and help me sew my costume. We already found a pattern I can use for my gown. It's simple but flattering."

"That's great," I replied, digging into my bag and procuring my script. "You'll still be walking around, even when you're not doing your puppet show, and it'll get some good use. And I bet you could reuse the dress for a Halloween party or something."

"That's a good idea!" With a smile, she flipped to a clean page in her notebook.

Students settled at the tables around us as Olivia and I spent the rest of the school day working on her play. It was easy for me to slip back into the dramatic work, shed my real-life concerns, and focus on something else. And it helped that Olivia was grateful for my assistance. She nodded and hmm'd as I offered ideas on how to rework passages for her puppet show.

The uneasy tension that had threaded between us started to unravel, slowly but surely. Maybe we were getting back to normal again. If she and I could maintain this, things would be great. I even found myself loosening up and laughing at her silly ideas on how to make the puppets exaggerate the romance and drama.

Plus, Jason was nowhere around us. Out of sight, out of mind.

Until the final bell rang. With it, my stomach started its mad fluttering again, reminding me of his words. He wanted to talk to me after school.

Thankfully, Olivia seemed oblivious to my nervousness. She gathered her stuff and crammed it into her backpack, shooting a grateful smile my way. "That was awesome. We got a lot of great work done, and I couldn't have done it without you. You have play practice tonight, right?"

I nodded.

"Have fun. I'll talk to you later, okay?" She waggled her fingers and swept out of the library, quickly weaving out of sight.

I closed my script and put it into my own bag, taking mental notes on what homework I needed to make up because of today's field trip.

"You heading home?" Jason said not a moment later from right behind me, appearing out of nowhere.

I jerked and looked up, giving him a small glare. "Stop scaring me like that," I whispered hotly. "And yes, I am."

He grinned, not put off in the least from my words. "Sorry 'bout that. Can I walk with you?" There was nothing upset or angry in his demeanor. He seemed casual, normal, totally at ease. At least whatever he had to talk about wasn't negative—or so it looked.

After standing and tossing my bag over my shoulder, I nodded in answer, my unease dissipating just a smidge in my stomach. In its place furled a little bit of warmth at our proximity. We made our way out of the library, down the hallway, out the front door. I was aware of his arm swinging lightly beside me, his long stride, the soft sounds of his breathing.

Most of the other students had already cleared out, so we were pretty much alone. Again.

A few minutes into our walk, Jason cleared his throat. "So, I need to ask you something."

And just like that, the nervous flutter in my stomach started again. "Um, sure," I said, trying to sound casual. "What is it?"

He paused, lightly touching my arm and stopping me right in front of him. His eyes were intense as they stared down at me. It took him a moment to finally speak. "Why do you dislike me so much?"

My jaw dropped; that was the last thing I'd expected to hear from him. "What?"

He glanced away, letting go of my arm and turning his attention just over my shoulder. "You've been very standoffish with me for a long time, and it's gotten worse since we started with play practice. I want to know why."

A couple of upper-class girls passed us on the sidewalk. I stayed quiet as their light whispers and laughs flitted on the breeze, waiting until they passed to speak. "What makes you think I don't like you?" I replied, knowing it was a ridiculous question but needing to hear his evidence.

He raised one eyebrow, looking back at me. "Come on. I'm not stupid. You either ignore me or you snip at me. You dislike when I give you any feedback on your acting, and you avoid me like the plague whenever you can."

I crossed my arms, flustered. Partly because he was right but also because it wasn't my fault I was always on guard with him. "If I *do* behave that way, it's only because you started it by—" I stopped.

Wow, I was about to tell him my vulnerable secret. How could I let that slip, and to him of all people?

"What? How did I start it?" There was an earnestness in his voice I hadn't heard before. A slight plea for answers.

I bit my lip. His gaze dropped down to look at my mouth, his own lips parting slightly. My cheeks blazed, remembering that intimate scene with him in the theater that I was trying so desperately to forget.

"Abbey," he said, the tone gentle. "Talk to me."

I swallowed. Should I fess up? Well, if he wanted me to tell, he should know. It wasn't my fault, after all—I'd done nothing wrong. "Do you remember freshman year's homecoming dance?"

Jason blinked in surprise. "Um, yeah."

"I . . . overheard something you said. About me." My face blazed. Curse my skin for being such a quick giveaway of my awkward misery. I turned away and looked at the stretch of sidewalk, sunlight dappling through leaves in splotchy patterns on the gray cement. My voice was flat as I continued. "You told one of your friends that I was boring. That you'd only dance with me if you wanted to get bored to death and that there was nothing interesting about me at all."

My words were met with a long stretch of silence. I refused to look at him, not wanting to see the emotion on his face. I wasn't sure I could handle it, whatever it was. Irritation. Impatience.

Or worse, even pity.

"Abbey," Jason finally whispered, regret thick in his voice. He touched my upper arm, fingers warm on my skin even through my sleeve, and guided me to look back at him. His bottomless eyes reflected every bit of depth in his tone. "I'm sorry. That was really unfair."

"You judged me without even knowing me," I said. My words were hot, the ache of mortification spilling out. "And I heard it. I heard you guys laughing at me." I yanked my arm out of his reach, struggling to maintain emotional control.

His lips pinched in reaction to my sudden distance. "I know. It was awful, and rude, and I've apologized. But you've been judging me this whole time too. Just because I made a big mistake and said something I shouldn't have doesn't mean that's how I always was . . . or am."

My jaw was clenched so tight it ached. I wanted to rail at him for what he said, but he was right. What I was doing was no better than what he'd done.

And he did apologize, after all. Refusing his apology was not only ungracious, it was unfair.

I relaxed my face, took a few breaths to unwind the tension from my stiffened body. "You're right. I've been just as biased about you as you were about me. And I apologize for that."

He looked at me then stuck out his hand.

I raised one eyebrow.

"Truce?" Jason gave me a crooked grin, an action that took away some of my frustration. He was silly, but earnest. "Please? Let's start completely over. I promise to not be a total jerk to you if you promise to not hold all of my mistakes against me forever and ever. Deal?"

I grabbed his hand and shook it once, firm. "Okay. Deal."

His thumb brushed against the top of my hand, leaving a trail of heat in its wake. I swallowed, heart slamming. One small touch reminded me just how much he impacted me. So very dangerous.

His eyes glinted; he crooked a grin. "I'm very much looking forward to our truce, Abbey."

I was too.

Heaven help me.

Chapter ● Eleven

The rest of the week was surprisingly decent. Since Jason and I had declared our tentative truce Monday after the field trip, things were much less dramatic between us. I found myself growing less sensitive to his feedback on my acting and instead taking it to heart.

He even showed me some ways to emote with my body and voice instead of relying upon my face to show what I was feeling. Mr. Ferrell seemed happy with our individual acting, though not quite as enthused with our onstage romance, saying in a slightly frustrated tone that we weren't giving it our all.

Thursday night's practice was grueling. He worked us all, running scenes again and again. Even the girls in the production were growing irritated with him . . . and with us. Practice ran over by a full half hour, with Mr. Ferrell growing increasingly crabby as he snapped at Jason and me about our awkward chemistry.

Probably because I was *totally* holding back.

Yeah, we'd come to some kind of peace, but that didn't stop this violent struggle of emotions within me. Now that he and I were no longer fighting, I was having a harder and harder time remembering why I'd disliked him in the first place. He was smart, witty, engaging—things I found myself continually drawn to.

And I was still struggling against showing it, sure that every feeling I experienced was plainly evident on my face, in spite of Mr. Ferrell's crabbiness. It was a delicate balance, one I was blowing big-time.

Our teacher finally ended practice, and everyone breathed a sigh of relief. "Hold on, Jason and Abbey," he said when we all started to clear the stage. "Stay back here. I need to talk to you for a few minutes."

I bit back a groan, shooting a skittish glance at Jason, who simply shrugged his shoulders in response.

Mr. Ferrell hopped onto the stage. He crossed his arms and studied us for so long I actually started to squirm.

"Mr. Ferrell?" I started tentatively. "Is . . . everything okay?"

A knowing smile grew on his face and he snapped his fingers. "Hmm. I think I know what's going on here."

I swallowed. *Oh no, he figured out that I like Jason. Please don't let him breathe a word about it*, I prayed.

"And what's that?" Jason asked.

"You two need to see a real couple in love."

My face erupted into flames. I cleared my throat and stared at the ground. The last thing I needed right now was anything to do with *that* word. Love. "Why do you think that?" I muttered.

"See?" he said, his voice growing excited as he talked. "Look how shy you are about it. You can't flinch from the emotion in our play, Abbey. Not if you're going to pull it off. You two are supposed to be falling in love, yet you're not convincing me." He paused. "But I think I know a way to help."

Jason remained silent; I didn't even risk a glance at him. But I did look up at Mr. Ferrell. "And how is that?"

"There's a production of *Romeo and Juliet* tomorrow night at the Beck Center in Lakewood. I have a friend who works there—he owes me a favor. I'll call in and have him put aside two tickets for you guys."

Friday night, out with Jason?

I swallowed again. "Um, I'm not sure we really need to do that," I said. "I just need to loosen up, is all."

Mr. Ferrell peered down at me. "You're not loosening up fast enough. Liana has great chemistry with Jason. You need to work harder on yours."

A flash of anger hit my chest. No way was she going to outshine me on this. I thrust my chin up. "Fine. I'll go see it. I'm sure my parents would be fine with it."

"Me too," Jason said smoothly.

I blinked, having almost forgotten he was there.

"Wonderful!" Mr. Ferrell clapped heartily, once again smiling. "The show is at eight. Be there a little early and go to will-call for your tickets. You'll love it. I know several of the actors in this production, and they're stellar. Absolutely amazing. Let me know what you think of it."

After giving a short nod, I grabbed my bag and headed to the theater doors, Jason right beside me. I had no idea what to say.

"Well, that was fun," he said drolly.

That broke the tension. "Nothing like hearing you're not being romantic enough to psych you out, huh?"

Our soft footsteps echoed in the hallway as we made our way to the front door of the school.

"Maybe I should work on batting my eyelashes more at you," Jason mused.

"I could giggle girlishly between my lines," I offered.

"I don't really see you as a giggling girl."

"I don't see you as a batting-your-eyelashes type of guy," I retorted.

"Guess I could be for you." He stopped and pressed a hand to his chest. "Forsooth, I must try harder." He swept into a low bow. "For milady, I will climb mountains and slay many dragons."

I curtsied, my hair flopping in my face. "And for my sir, I will . . . um . . . slay the leftover dragons, I suppose."

He rose, a bright laugh in his eyes. "We are quite a pair, aren't we."

My pulse picked up, throbbing at my wrists and throat. "I suppose we are. Hopefully, this play will be good."

We went through the door and made it outside. The sun was low in the sky, barely a splash of pink on the horizon. The air was tinged a bit cooler, and I shivered.

Before I knew it, a light jacket was wrapped around my shoulders. "Here," Jason said. "You looked chilly."

I bit my lip and breathed in; it smelled like him, and the sensation wrapped around me. "That was nice of you. Thanks."

He chuckled. "You can give it back tomorrow night. At the play, I mean."

Our non-date date. Oh, God, was I ready for this? To sit beside him for two to three hours, smelling him and feeling the heat of his body beside me, pretending the only feeling I had for him was innocent friendship?

"—can take us," he was saying.

"Um, what? Sorry, I . . . I didn't hear," I stammered.

"I'm sure my mom can take us," he enunciated. "Want me to say it again, but slower this time?"

I swatted his arm. "Smarty-pants."

"That's what they tell me."

I slipped my arms into the sleeves. The jacket was slightly bigger, cocooning me in its warmth. We approached a fork in the sidewalk. "Well, I'm going this way," I said slowly, suddenly wanting to prolong the moment.

"And I'm going this way," he said, pointing to the right fork.

"Then you should head that way," I teased back. "Or someone might wonder what happened to you."

"I'll see you tomorrow, Abbey." With that smoky-whispered promise, Jason sauntered off, leaving me watching him retreat.

My whole walk home, all I could think about was him.

Friday night, I stared at myself in the full-length mirror hanging on the back of my door, trying to study all possible sides of my body. My head berated me for being so ridiculous—it wasn't a date. We were going as friends.

Colleagues, really. Just taking in a show, learning from other actors. A professional gathering.

But my heart wouldn't stop racing, and my palms were sweating like it was a thousand degrees in my room.

After changing outfits a good half-dozen times, I'd finally settled on a jean skirt and pale-pink dressy shirt, paired with flats. The shirt sleeves were slitted, allowing little peeks of my arms to show through. Understated but cute.

Not that it mattered what he thought, right?

"Abbey, he's here," my mom hollered from downstairs.

My heart rate picked up again, kicking into double time.

Caroline peeked her head in the door, a massive grin nearly splitting her face in two. "You look adorable, sis. Are you nervous?"

I swiped a palm down the front of my shirt, smoothing it. "Of course not. There's nothing to be nervous about." The slight tremble in my voice gave me away, and given the way Caroline's grin got even wider, she totally picked up on it.

"Uh-huh," she said in a dry tone, slipping inside my bedroom and circling around me a couple of times, taking in my outfit with careful scrutiny. "You look nice. Now, you have enough money, right?"

I nodded. Jason had said his parents were planning on taking his little brother out to a movie while we went to our play, so we'd all grab a quick bite to eat before the production, and they'd pick us up when it was done. So not only were we going to the play, we were also hanging out with his family. I was pretty sure that was the point I'd started getting really nervous about tonight.

"Just play it cool. You'll be fine." She squeezed my shoulder. Her voice softened as she continued, "You look really pretty, Abbey. He'd be a total idiot not to notice you tonight."

I gave her a small hug. My sister wasn't the warmest person ever, but she knew the right thing to say when I needed to hear it. She also knew that despite my protests, tonight was more important to me than I'd let on. "Thanks."

"Okay, you'd better get downstairs, before Mom starts asking him too many questions." She chuckled, probably having gone through that a time or ten since she'd started dating last year.

Crap, she was right. I grabbed my purse and almost ran down the stairs.

Then stopped.

Jason was there, wearing a pair of black pants and a slim black dress shirt. He looked tall, lean, totally commanding my attention. "Hey," he said, sound a little throaty as he took in my outfit. "You look great."

Mom beamed at him, dropping back from his side so I could join him in the living room. "Okay, you two be careful and have fun." She walked over to the window and waved at what I assume was his parents' car. "Nice people—they popped in here quickly to meet me."

My throat grew even drier when Jason took my hand to lead me to the door. "Um, 'kay, Mom," I managed to say.

And then we were out in the balmy May air, a light breeze fluttering my shirt.

We made it to the bottom of the stairs when I stopped in my tracks. "Crud. I forgot your jacket. Hold on."

He tugged my hand. "Oh, we can get it another time. Don't worry about it."

Was he just in a rush to leave, or was there the off chance he possibly want me to keep it and didn't know how to tell me? I couldn't tell from his face or his voice. But it didn't matter anyway. He was practically dragging me toward the car.

He opened my door—yes, I admit I melted a little—and let me in behind the driver's seat. His brother was sitting in the middle, wearing a big smile as he waved at me. Then Jason ran over to his side and hopped in.

Jason's mom and dad turned around and faced me, beaming.

"Hi!" his mom said, turning on the dome light and flooding

the car interior in a golden glow. She was surprisingly young, with no gray in her hair that I could see, and she had on low jeans and a T-shirt. She thrust her hand out. "I'm Jillian. It's great to meet you. Jason has told us all about you."

I dared a teasing glance at him. "I wouldn't believe a word of it. He's notoriously shifty, as I'm sure you know."

Instead of smirking, the way I thought he would, his cheeks burned bright red, and he swallowed then looked away.

Was he nervous? Something in my chest cracked and softened into a pile of butter. Suddenly I felt less nervous, less unsure. If he was nervous, I wasn't the only one putting pressure on tonight. And, oddly enough, I found comfort in that solidarity. He wanted it to go well too.

Jason's dad was shaved completely bald; the look worked well on him. He winked at me. "Well, he told us you were really cute . . ."

"Dad," Jason said in a low voice. "Stop."

His parents chuckled in the front seat, and his mom turned off the dome light. "Okay, honey," she said. "I'll stop torturing you. For now."

I turned my attention to Braedon, wanting to give Jason a minute or two to relax and also needing the time myself. "So, what movie are you going to see?"

He wiggled in his booster seat. "Mom said we were going to see *Carly Coral.* She's a coral in the ocean who wants to see the world. It's a cartoon, and she told me if I was good and did all my work this week, she'd take me." His face was completely serious, as though we were talking politics instead of an animated film.

"That sounds great," I said solemnly. "You'll have to let us know how it is. Jason and I are going to see a play."

"I heard," he said. "Jason was talking about it with one of his friends, and—"

Jason clapped a hand over his brother's mouth. "That's enough about that," he said, giving a nervous chuckle.

"Why, Jason, I really wanted to hear what your brother had to say," I said in fake admonition.

He shot Braedon a warning look, and the boy responded with a nod. Jason took his hand off his mouth. "Anyway," he said loudly, "it's going to be a great play. I'm looking forward to it."

"Is there kissing?" Braedon made a scrunched-up face with so much misery that I couldn't help but laugh.

"A little," I responded. "But it's a tragic romance."

"What is tragic?" he asked innocently.

Ah, crap. No way could I explain to him that Romeo and Juliet died in the end. "Um, well . . ." I shot a desperate look at Jason.

"It ends sadly," he said smoothly, saving my hide. "They don't stay together."

I nodded. "Yup. Sad."

The rest of the car ride went quickly, as did dinner. Jason's parents were funny, with that dry, smartmouthed humor I could easily see he got from them. I instantly felt comfortable with them, and they seemed interested in me, asking lots of questions about my classes and extracurricular activities while we shared a spinach-dip appetizer and I noshed on my quesadilla.

If only I weren't so hyperaware of Jason. He sat on my right, his thigh pressed against mine. My bottom half was practically frozen in place, my leg nearly seared by the contact of his.

Either he wasn't feeling it, or he didn't notice. He seemed completely casual, laughing and talking. I made a good effort to do the same and distract myself from him.

When we finished dinner, I took out a twenty to cover my food, but his dad waved it away, refusing to take it. Really nice people, and a secret part of me hoped that maybe in the future, there might be a reason to be around them more.

Jason's mom dropped us in front of the Beck Center twenty minutes before the start of the show. People were filtering in, lingering out front, hanging in the lobby and looking at artwork I could see through the large glass windows.

"Jason, send me a text when the play's over," she said then gave him a hug. She glanced over at me, giving an enigmatic smile that lit up her eyes, so similar to Jason's. "You guys have lots of fun."

Chapter ● Twelve

The play was thrilling.

I'd never seen acting quite so engaging, so emotional as this production of *Romeo and Juliet*. After the first act, I could see why Mr. Ferrell felt Jason and I needed to work on our acting skills. It humbled and embarrassed me to realize just how much I still needed to learn about the craft.

The actors moved across the stage like liquid, flowing and ebbing with emotion. Their faces, their voices, their very bodies breathed life into words that freshman year had fallen flat for me on paper.

Plus, the theater itself was nice—much bigger than ours, yet cozier, too, in a way.

Jason sat beside me, rapt as well. His face was filled with

concentration as he studied the actors, likely noting techniques and ideas he should implement. It was equally fascinating watching those thoughts flicker across his face. I could tell by the way he squinted his eyes, how he rubbed a hand along the back of his neck while scrutinizing the play.

I shifted in the narrow seat, my leg brushing against his for the hundredth time since we'd sat down. "Sorry," I whispered, fighting as hard as I could to ignore the tingles across my skin. "These seats are tiny."

He turned to look at me, the stage light casting a glow across half his face. "Stop blaming the seats. I know you're just trying to touch me."

I gave him a mock scowl and whispered, "Darn. You figured out my sinister scheme. I made sure we'd get sent here by Mr. Ferrell and put in the tiniest seats in the universe, just so I could 'accidentally' touch you."

I thought I heard him say, "I'll make sure to thank Mr. Ferrell," but I couldn't be certain if that was real or just a tiny bit of wishful thinking. And I sure didn't want to ask him to clarify.

During intermission, we got up and wandered around, checking out the amateur artwork on the walls. It was totally cool the way the center supported local students. Today's display featured photographs of Cleveland sites, both color and black and white. I recognized several famous statues and buildings, like the downtown library and Severance Hall, where the Cleveland Orchestra performed.

"You should submit something of yours," Jason said. "So it can be on display."

I blinked. "Really? You think so?"

"I saw your final from art class last year in the hallway. It was good. Really good. You have an amazing eye for composition."

My face heated with pleasure. "That's . . . really nice of you to say," I whispered. "Thanks."

"Don't thank me for telling the truth." He stopped, rubbing the back of his neck again, a frown creasing his face this time. He pulled me to a corner, away from the rest of the milling crowd. "Abbey, I was really unfair to judge you so harshly last year. It's still eating away at me. I know we talked about it earlier this week, but I haven't been able to stop thinking about it since then. I hurt your feelings. I never wanted to be 'that guy'—the one who didn't care about what other people felt."

My breath caught in my throat as he captured me in his gaze.

"I'm so sorry I was a jerk," he continued. "It wasn't even true, you know. When I saw your photos last year, I got a bit of a hint that I'd been too rash in assuming those things about you." He paused, looking at the ground. His voice was tight. "I was stubborn and not ready to admit I was wrong. But now I can admit it, and I do. There's nothing boring about you, Abbey. Not at all."

My heart swelled. Before I could stifle the impulse, I reached out and took his hand, meaning to squeeze it in a friendly, forgiving gesture. But the moment my fingers slid against his, I lost what I was going to say.

Jason looked up in surprise then tugged me closer. We were only a few inches apart. So very, very close. Electricity practically crackled between our bodies.

The lights flickered off, on, off, on.

I laughed. Couldn't help it—figured that such a perfect moment would be interrupted. His face split into a grin as well.

"Time for part two," he said, a wry grin on his face.

As I followed him into the theater and back to our seats, I couldn't help but think we were also on part two of our relationship, whatever it was. Something had changed between us.

And all I could think was that I wanted more.

I spent the rest of the weekend avoiding talking to Olivia about anything to do with Jason or the play. It was awful, and I couldn't stop the guilty twinge in my gut when I thought about how I was "seeing" Jason behind her back. Yes, Mr. Ferrell had asked us to go, so it wasn't a real date.

But as much as I tried to rationalize it, I knew the truth.

I'd *wanted* it to be a date. Wanted it so badly that at the end of the night, when Jason's parents had dropped me off, I'd been painfully self-conscious saying good night to him, not wanting it to end, lingering on my front step with him for way too long. But Jason took my awkwardness in stride, giving me his trademark smile and telling me he'd see me on Monday.

I couldn't stop replaying that intermission scene in my mind either and had lain in bed long after coming home Friday night thinking about it. There was something in the earnestness of his words, the way he'd looked into my eyes. I was starting to think that maybe Jason was getting some kind of a spark of a feeling for me too.

And if Olivia knew about that, knew that we'd gone out together—regardless of the reason—it would damage our friendship. Maybe even permanently, especially once she realized I'd lied about liking him.

So I'd stayed quiet about it. Hadn't even told her. And the guilt was eating away at my insides.

Lucky for me, she'd not pushed me to talk, even when coming over for our regular Saturday dinner and movie night. I'd popped in a funny action flick because I knew it would keep Olivia laughing and occupied . . . and her mind off romance.

I was the worst friend.

Monday morning, I trudged my way to school, bleary-eyed. I hadn't slept much Saturday night or last night, guilt keeping me awake far too long. Combined with Friday night's "daydreaming" about Jason, I was running on empty.

I sipped my coffee from my travel mug—overflowing with sugar and creamer, just the way I liked it—and tried to shake off the sleepiness. *Come on, caffeine*, I prayed. *Do your thing.*

After all, I was heading to gym class, where I was gonna have to get sweaty and work out . . . and see Jason.

That sure got my heart racing. I swigged the coffee, finishing it in record time, and made it to the girls' changing room. Lauretta was already in there, slipping into her bright-orange gym shorts, which clashed with her neon-green T-shirt. The girl didn't care at all about matching colors, but somehow the look worked on her.

She glanced over at me, smiling. Her hair was no longer high-lighted but now a pale blond, making her skin appear even more delicate and perfect. "There you are. You look sleepy."

I shrugged. "Coffee will kick in soon. Just waiting."

"Have a good weekend?"

I plopped down on the bench and reached over to my tiny gym locker, digging out my stuff and changing quickly. "I did. Went to see *Romeo and Juliet* on Friday at the Beck Center. It was awesome."

"Oh, that sounds fun!" She paused then looked at me, tilting her head. Her eyes slitted into a suspicious look. "And who did we go with, hmm?"

I glanced away. "It was a school thing. Mr. Ferrell had asked us to go, so we went because we knew it would help the play. That was all. No big deal." The way I was continuing to ramble was a dead giveaway.

"Oh my gosh," she whispered. "You're kidding. You went with Jason, didn't you. Was it a date?"

"Not at all," I declared, tugging my hair into a ponytail.

"I want to know everything," she retorted. "Tell me—"

"Girls, stop gabbing and get outside." Mrs. Belati interrupted Lauretta. She popped her curly head through the door, waving at us and a couple of other stragglers. "Let's go, let's go!"

For once, I was happy for the distraction of gym. Until I saw Jason, stretching and warming up off to the side by himself.

Lauretta leaned over. "You're going to tell me everything. Don't think you've dodged me."

I chuckled. "You sound scary."

She tried to fight the smirk on her face but lost. "Um, I am scary. Don't forget it, lady."

"Do three laps around the field and then come back here," Mrs. Belati hollered to our class.

A lot of groans, but we all made our way to the track, slogging through laps. Jason stayed with his friends, not dashing by me in a challenge, and I fought the urge to run up to him and dare him to beat me. My head was all mixed up. I needed to stop thinking about him.

Lauretta and I poked along until we were in the back of the group. "So," she huffed, jogging along beside me, "you like him."

I nodded, not trusting myself to speak.

"And you're finally admitting it to yourself."

Another nod.

"That's so cute," she said. "I've been waiting forever for this moment."

"Hardy har," I replied.

"No, seriously. With the intensity crackling between you two, it's a wonder you guys haven't started dating yet. The glances he throws you when you're not looking are hot enough to fry an egg."

"That sounds attractive," I said with a laugh.

We turned the corner.

"I'm guessing you haven't shared any of this with Olivia," she continued.

My heart lurched, thudded painfully. "No, and it's best to keep it that way. Nothing is going to happen between me and Jason. I'm just coming to terms with the fact that I don't despise him anymore. But that's it for us."

No matter how much I wanted to think otherwise.

Lauretta and I jogged in silence to finish this lap, then the next. When we started lap three, she said, "You know, there's a party this weekend at my cousin Jennifer's house. It's her eighteenth birthday, and practically everyone from the school will be there. You should come with me."

"I don't want to intrude," I said.

"No, seriously. You won't be." We rounded the first curve. "She told me to ask my friends. They have a huge place. Plus, cake." She grabbed my arm, widening her eyes. "*Cake*, Abbey. You can't miss out on that. My mom said it was going to be big enough to feed fifty people. That's practically a wedding-size feast."

I chuckled. "Gosh, when you put it that way . . ."

She lowered her voice and leaned in, her breath huffing against my ear. "Jennifer also hired a band to play. They're supposed to be really good."

"Oh, really?" I wasn't sure why that was so secret-worthy, but okay.

"Jason's the bassist."

I stumbled over my feet and righted myself, glancing around to make sure no one caught my clumsiness. "Seriously?"

Jason was going to be at this party. Olivia hadn't mentioned it at all, which meant she probably wasn't going to go. Or that she didn't know about it.

It might be an opportunity for me to see Jason in a more casual environment, one without the pressures and strains of school and the play. I could see if this new side of him was genuine or a front. Because surely he'd be around his friends too.

"I'll think about it," I finally said.

She grinned, knowing she had me, that I'd be there. "Wear something supercute. I'm interested in seeing what exactly is going to happen on Friday night when the two of you are together. You know, for scientific reasons."

I snorted. "Yeah, science. I'm sure."

One thing I knew: Friday night was going to be very interesting.

Chapter ● Thirteen

You have wounded me, milady," Jason said in mock disappointment, gliding across the stage floor toward me. His eyes were alight with a sparkle of a laugh as he drew closer to me.

I glanced away from him toward the empty seats, licking my lips and putting on a wicked smile. "One cannot wound a person who has no heart, can she? And after all the other women you've cast aside over the years, methinks it a fair assessment to make such a proclamation about you."

Jason grabbed my hand, and instant warmth shot through that limb, leaving my skin tingling. "Rosalyn, I cannot bear the way you tease me."

"Bear it, you must," I chided. "For it is no different than the teasing you gave me since childhood."

Funny how closely the lines of the play echoed our reality. Only I wasn't quite so sore about the parts that had made me sore before. Everything was changing, and each time he and I evolved, it impacted the way I felt toward him in the play.

Made me softer, flirtier. Less abrasive.

I slid from his grasp and took two steps back. He took two steps toward me, the gleam in his eyes positively wicked.

"Only you know the real me," he said passionately, grabbing my hand again. "Even my own flesh and blood doesn't understand me the way you do. Only you—"

His phone vibrated.

He blinked and let my hand go, grabbing the cell out of his pocket and looking down. Luckily it was only our private Monday practice, not our group rehearsal, or Mr. Ferrell would have flayed him alive for keeping his phone in his pocket.

"Crud. It's my brother," he said, breaking character. "Sorry, hold on a sec," he said, giving me an apologetic look and stepping away to the far side of the stage. "Hey, Braedon. What's up?"

I tried not to eavesdrop, but the look of concern mixed with frustration on his face made me unable to tune them out.

"Bud, I can't. I'm practicing right now. Remember the play I told you about? Our big performance is in a couple of weeks, and I . . . yes, I know." He sighed, glanced at me, and rolled his eyes. "Yes, she's here with me. No, she's . . ."

Was his brother talking about me? My pulse picked up in a nervous flutter. What were they talking about?

Jason sighed again. "Okay, okay. Hold on. I'll be home soon." He shut his phone off and moved back over toward me. "Braedon's freaking out right now because my mom isn't home yet, and he doesn't like the next-door neighbor watching him. He wants me to come home."

I swallowed back my disappointment and gave him a forgiving smile. "Oh, okay. Well, we've made great progress, so don't worry about it."

"He's getting really clingy lately, and I'm not sure why." His brow marred. "He's not normally like this. I'm sorry. I feel really bad. We were getting in a great groove with the practice."

On impulse, I laid my hand on his upper arm. The slender muscles beneath were tight, rigid; he was frustrated and torn, the emotion clearly splaying across his face. "Seriously, it's okay, Jason. We're pretty much off the script now for most of our scenes. With the progress we're making, we'll have this down in no time, I guarantee you. Go home and hang out with him. It sounds like he's a little insecure because you're not home as much as you used to be."

He stepped closer, looking down at me. "You think so?"

I nodded. "I babysat my cousin for the whole summer last year. When school started again, she called me constantly, asking me to come over, telling me she wished I lived with her. She'd gotten used to me being around. It's flattering, actually. Braedon must think a lot of you."

Something about that warmed my heart all the more. His

brother obviously loved him enough to be upset when he wasn't around. A sentiment I couldn't blame the kid for, as I found myself unable to stop thinking about him too.

"Maybe you can let him visit with us here while we practice," I continued. "He might enjoy that. He won't feel so left out, and we can still get some work done."

A slow smile spread across his face. "You're pretty smart, you know that?"

I shrugged, my face flushed. Then I realized I was still holding his arm and let it go, the flush on my cheeks getting hotter. "That's what my teachers keep telling me."

It was refreshing and fun to dish the bravado back out to him, the way he constantly did to me. There was an intimacy to our acquaintance that was evolving into a rich friendship. Of course, every time we got closer—physically and emotionally—it made me feel things I shouldn't be feeling.

Made me want things I shouldn't be wanting, too.

"I should get going anyway," I blurted out, heading toward the theater seats and grabbing my backpack and purse. "I have a lot of homework today. My teachers were extracruel for a Monday."

He laughed, dropping down off the stage to grab his backpack. "Well, don't let me stand in the way."

With footsteps in sync, he and I made our way through the theater doors, down the empty school hallway, a habit becoming far too familiar. Comforting. Yet still zinged with a thread of excitement, a knowledge that there was something unusual between us. Jason and I walked outside. The sun was covered over by a smattering of clouds, but the air was still pleasant, even if a little on the brisk side.

We made it to the fork in the sidewalk, where we always went our separate ways, me heading to my house and him to his.

"Have fun with your brother," I finally said, wishing we could stand here longer but knowing he had to go. "And tell him I said hi."

"I will." He paused, looked like he wanted to say more.

"What is it?"

Clearing his throat, he looked away. "Oh, nothing. It's nothing. See you tomorrow, Abbey." With that, he walked off.

The whole way home, I couldn't help but wonder what he'd wanted to say . . . and why he'd stopped himself from talking. Jason was always free-speaking, hardly one to censor himself.

I shrugged it off and headed home, thoughts of his smile warming me from the inside out.

Exhaling in frustration, I slammed my biology book closed and plopped back on my bed. I was tired of the musculoskeletal system, unable to focus. Mind flitting about like a hummingbird.

There was a light rap on my door. "It's me," Caroline said, her voice muffled through the door.

"Come in." I sat up and shoved the books into a pile on the floor.

Caroline slipped inside, holding two mugs of steaming tea,

and closed the door with her foot. She handed me a mug, which I took with a grateful sigh, perching on the edge of my bed and wrapping her hands around her mug.

"What's up, sis?" she asked.

I raised one eyebrow. This was very unlike her, to come in and make small talk with me. Caroline was usually too busy hanging out with her friends to give me the time of day. "Not much. You?" I didn't like the way the cautiousness came out in my voice but couldn't help it.

Fortunately she didn't seem offended. "Mom sent me in here," she said with a chuckle. "She's worried about you."

I was both disappointed and relieved at this revelation. "She did? Why?"

Caroline shrugged, her blond hair shifting lightly on her slender shoulders. "She said you seem a little . . . off. Plus, with you going out with that guy—"

"It wasn't a date," I protested, wrapping my own fingers around the mug to draw a little of its warmth into my suddenly chilly hands.

She raised a hand. "Whoa, I know that. But Mom just wants to make sure you're okay, and she's afraid of looking too nosy."

"Which is why she sent you to do her dirty work," I finished with a laugh. "That sounds about right."

"Her methods are sketchy, but she means well." Caroline sipped her tea leisurely, then continued, "So, is everything okay with you? Really? I won't talk to her about it, promise."

126

Something in her voice seemed genuine. And the look in her eyes showed real interest in me. It had been so long since we'd talked, really talked, that I found myself opening my mouth to spill the beans.

So I told her everything, without holding back—last year's homecoming debacle, the play, Jason, Olivia, *Romeo and Juliet*, our near-kiss, the whole nine yards. When I finished, I took several draws on my tea as she sat and pondered my gut-purging confession.

"Every day, I feel more and more guilty," I said. "It's spiraling out of control. I can't help the way I'm feeling about him, no matter how I try to fight it. But Olivia likes him too. I can't do anything about my feelings. She means too much to me."

Caroline popped her mug on my bedside table and leaned against my headboard, draping a pillow across her lap. "You're in quite a pickle here," she mused.

"You're telling me," I said drolly.

"Seems to me like there's a few different issues going on here. One, you like Jason. You can't help how you feel about him—and there's nothing wrong with that." She took a big drink of her tea. "You're far too smart to like someone who isn't worthy of your heart or your attention."

I flushed from the compliment.

"It also sounds like Jason's starting to like you, too."

I sat up a bit, stared at her. "You think so?"

She crooked an eyebrow. "Sis, he's throwing off signals left and right. Just because you're not picking them up doesn't mean they're not there."

"Like what?"

"Going out with you to *Romeo and Juliet*—and no, I don't want to hear that it wasn't a 'date.' Because it was, even if you don't want to admit it. The near-kisses. The way he looks at you, which I saw for myself on Friday when I peeked at him before you two left. Need I go on?"

I kind of wanted her to, but I shook my head, not wanting to look needy. "I think I get your point."

"Okay." She shifted until she sat cross-legged against the headboard. "So there's that. Regarding Olivia, here's what I believe wholeheartedly. You have nothing to worry about or apologize for."

"You think?" Something in my chest loosened up just a bit upon hearing her words. I so desperately wanted to stop feeling guilty.

"You and Jason haven't done anything. As far as anyone knows, you're friends. In the same way Olivia can't help her feelings, you can't help your feelings either. The difference is, you're conscientious about not wanting to hurt her, whereas she's being insecure and taking it out on you."

I bristled a bit at the dig against Olivia, ready to defend her.

"Whoa, whoa," she said, holding up a hand. "Before you get upset, let me clarify. I didn't mean that she doesn't care about your feelings. I mean that somewhere deep inside her, she suspects she never had a chance with Jason . . . and she may also suspect that you did. In fact, that you *do*. And she's trying to process this— albeit not the best way, in my opinion."

I nodded, slightly mollified. "But what do we do about it? I mean, I *can't* tell her how I feel about him. And right now it doesn't even matter. He's not asking me out or making it clear if he likes me. So what would be the point in confessing to her?"

"At some point, things are going to hit the fan, Abbey." She sipped her tea, finishing the last of the cup. "Either you're going to remain friends with Jason, or he's going to take that last step and declare his feelings. And then you have a few decisions to make."

If he did, would I date him?

If he did, how would I tell Olivia?

My gut pinched. This was so complicated. The easy path would be to stay friends with Jason, of course. But it would also be ignoring that part of my heart that grew a little bit bigger every day. The part that wanted to be more than friends with him.

But acting on that would likely hurt Olivia so badly, we might never recover from the fallout.

I looked down into my mug and sighed.

"I know, sis. It's no fun dealing with guys, is it." Her voice was soft, empathetic.

"Have you ever had something like this happen to you?" I asked her.

"Hmm. No, not quite. A friend and I were both interested in the same guy earlier this year."

I looked up. "What happened?"

She grinned. "He turned out to be a jerk, so we both dropped him. No love lost there."

I shook my head, chuckling. That didn't help my situation, but it was good to see this wasn't a unique problem. That friends ran into this kind of thing at times.

Her face turned serious. "Abbey, if Jason asks you out and you want to be his girlfriend, at some point you're going to have to tell Olivia exactly how you feel. It's not going to be fun. But if she's a real friend, she'll get over it and still care about you. You're not poaching him—they don't have anything beyond a casual friendship, so there's nothing to poach."

"I know," I whispered, gnawing on my lower lip. "But I still feel bad, like I'm doing something wrong. She's liked him for a long time."

Given how much Olivia had backed away from me over the last couple of weeks just because of the possibility of me liking Jason, if anything ever really *did* happen between him and me, it would be a hundred times worse.

"But she doesn't know him," Caroline retorted. "She knows *of* him, what she sees in class. The same as you used to. But you know him now, in a way she doesn't. You guys are genuine. Her feelings are just a crush." She peered at me then stood, dropping my pillow back on the bed. "And I think we both know that what you're feeling goes well beyond a crush."

I chewed my lip another moment and nodded. She was right.

And while I wanted to believe what she was telling me, I was petrified. Olivia was my best friend, flaws and all. If a guy came between us, if she cut me off because of it, there would be a hole in my heart no one else could fill.

All I could do was tread water as carefully as possible for now . . . and hope that whatever happened, things would turn out okay.

Chapter ♥ Fourteen

Rosalyn . . ." Jason took my hand and drew me to center stage, where the lighting guy changed the light to focus on the two of us in a bright, glowing beam. "I can't live without you. I . . . I love you."

Jason's eyes burned with an intensity I wasn't sure was entirely just acting, flickering with layers of emotion that pulled me toward him. Regardless of whether it was truth or fiction, it left me breathless and practically shaking in his arms.

A good thing, since my character was supposed to be swooning big-time. Not so hard to fake at all.

Drawing in a breath to steady myself, I pressed a hand to my chest, the memorized words at the end of the play coming easily to my lips by now. I blinked rapidly and turned my face from him. "Wait, you . . . you love me? But how can this be?

You have done nothing but tease and torture me from childhood on. Our whole history is built upon this strange antagonism between us."

Jason chuckled, clenching my hand tighter. Was I going crazy, or did I detect a slight shake in his hand too? I had to be imagining it, right? "From the first time I pulled your hair at the side of the river," he said on a soft breath, "I knew I loved you. How could I not? Especially when you returned my attention with a punch in the nose—well deserved, I might add."

I grinned at first in response to his teasing commentary, then creased my brow in confusion and proceeded slowly to the far end of the stage, where I could see Mr. Ferrell nodding his approval. His face was stern, fixed, but not critical. . . . He was intently into the play.

A rush of success swept through me as I continued my lines. "I never knew you felt that way. Why did you not speak of these feelings before . . . before your brother made his intentions clear toward me?"

Jason slipped behind me and took my hand, turning me to face him. His eyes sparkled with regret and other emotions I couldn't quite place. "Would you have trusted me, had you known?" He shook his head. "I have railed against this for far too long, believe me. My heart did struggle with the knowledge that I could not let my brother win your hand. Not when . . . when I wanted it for my own. I could no longer remain silent."

I stepped closer to him until we were so close, I could see the flecks of dark brown in his irises. "Oh, my dear William, I love you too."

Our lips drew closer, closer . . . and I froze.

I was mesmerized by his eyes, unable to look away. And I was stiff with fear, knowing that if I moved my mouth closer to his, pressed my warm lips against his, the naked truth of my ever-increasing feelings would be laid bare before him, before Mr. Ferrell, before all the other cast and crew.

And I was so not ready for that.

So instead, I gave a nervous giggle and backed away slightly, scrambling for some kind of a save.

Jason's eyebrow quirked up, though his eyes stayed intensely locked on mine. Fortunately he didn't seem offended by my strangeness, as if he recognized that I needed a moment.

"What's wrong?" Mr. Ferrell asked.

"Um, well," I started, my face flaming so hard I was sure my cheeks were going to combust, "I'm not sure I'm . . ."

Desperate, I cast a nervous glance around me.

"Mr. Ferrell," Jason interjected, "I think we just need a moment." He guided me by the elbow to the back of the stage. "What's wrong?"

There was no way I could tell him the truth. I grappled for the right words to say, spewing out, "I just . . . I wonder if it might be better for us to wait to . . . you know, to kiss during the actual play. For authenticity, so if it's the real first time, it'll come across that way. To the audience." I couldn't stop my babbling words and wanted to stuff a rag in my mouth.

He tilted his head, studied me. "If that's what you want, that's fine. We can wait on it." There was a bit of a flatness in his voice. Or maybe I was simply imagining it, secretly hoping he'd be disappointed.

A realization that became even more convincing when he swept across the stage and said with no flatness whatsoever, "Mr. Ferrell, we're gonna wait and skip the kiss until opening day. It'll be more authentic that way."

"Hmm." Our teacher rubbed his jaw. "Interesting. Worth a shot. If you guys keep giving it your all like you did today, it should work out fine. I'm really feeling the chemistry between you two now."

Despite my embarrassment, I found myself flushing again—with pleasure this time. Was it the *Romeo and Juliet* outing that had helped us be more fluid and natural around each other?

Was it something growing between us?

Whatever was the cause, it was working.

Mr. Ferrell clapped. "Okay, let's go back to the beginning of the last act. Noblemen, please take your places onstage. Ladies, line up across from them for the dance scene. Rosalyn and William, you can exit now. Thanks for your hard work."

Off the hook . . . at least for a while. Until the day of the play, when I'd be forced to face the music and kiss Jason.

We took our seats in the front and grabbed our scripts, our habit when we weren't onstage. My eyes read the script, my mouth breathed the lines, but my brain was completely detached.

All I could think about was Jason's lips, the way his fresh cologne floated around me every time he stepped near me. The glint of stage lights across his hair.

I was getting so caught up in him, way past anything I could control. And even crazier, I found myself liking this rush. This fall headfirst into . . . whatever it was. The emotions saturated me, made colors brighter, made everything just a little bit warmer in my life.

If this was a crush, how had I lived without it this long? No wonder Olivia was so adamant to cling to this feeling. It made everything in life so much more vivid and worth experiencing.

I huffed a small exhale at the thought of my best friend.

"What's going on?" Jason asked me in a low whisper.

I shook my head. "Oh, nothing I can't handle. You know, just everyday stress." Yeah, nothing big, except that the more I found myself falling for Jason, the greater my risk for losing my best friend.

Wednesday evening, Olivia and I were parked on her basement floor, surrounded by yards of clipped fabric, ribbons of all shapes and colors, and spools of thread as far as the eye could see.

"This gown is going to be amazing," Olivia breathed. She stood and pressed the rich green velvet fabric to the front of her waist, where it fell in soft pleats just below her feet. The color highlighted the fair tone of her skin. "And since the pattern is super simple, I'm definitely going to have it done before the faire. Yay!"

I gave her a massive heartfelt smile, happy to be focusing for a little while on something other than guy issues. It was good to spend fun time with my best friend, especially when she was relaxed and grinning. The way things used to be before everything got crazy complicated. "You are going to have the prettiest dress at the Ren faire. I guarantee it."

I looked down at my own bloodred dress. It was a heavy satin that draped nicely on me and fit like a glove. When shopping with my mom yesterday, I'd found a simple shell that I was adding on to with various fabrics and embellishments. Tugging the thread from the neckline, I snipped it off.

"Mine's not quite coming along as I'd hoped," I continued wryly. "Oh, well." It would be done before the faire so long as I continued to work regularly on it.

"Here," Olivia said, shoving a box of miscellaneous sewing material at me. "I have some pretty lace hiding somewhere in the bottom that you can add around the sleeves if you want."

I beamed at her. "Thanks!" I dug through the box, finding the roll of lace. "Oh, this is perfect. How's your puppet play coming along, anyway?"

"It's great." Olivia bit off a strand of thread at the hem, tugging on it to make sure it was secure. "I finished writing it last night. I think it's gonna be funny. Can we get together next week to make the puppets?"

"Oh, that is gonna be hilarious," I said, shaking my head with a chuckle. "Are you going to make them look like us?"

She shrugged. "Why not? That would be even funnier, I think."

"I'm definitely in." I stretched the lace around my sleeve and snipped off the excess then grabbed my needle and white thread and began to tack it to the edge. "I wonder how the other projects are coming along."

Most of our World History class time was now filled up with talking about the Renaissance faire. Plans were being tossed out left and right about how to organize booths, scheduling for special events and features, and the like. There was going to be a group of wandering minstrels, some gypsies and fortune-tellers, and a couple of kids were learning how to juggle.

Serious fun. I was getting more excited just thinking about it.

"So, how's play practice?" Olivia asked.

I froze up just a tiny bit but forced myself to relax my shoulders and back. "Great. I have almost all of the lines memorized," I said lightly. "Which is good, because Liana has been eyeballing me closely lately. I think she's hoping I'll get sick."

"You might want to watch your lunches," she said with a laugh. "Didn't people used to get poisoned through their food back then? Like, sprinkled on top of their turkey *legges* or something?"

I snorted. "She'd have to stay awake long enough to come up with a plan, much less execute it."

In spite of Liana's longing gazes at Jason throughout every

single practice, she still didn't manage to remain conscious in class. If she had even one act memorized of the play, I'd be floored.

"Any good plans this weekend?" I asked her casually. We still hadn't talked about the party so I needed to find out if she was planning to go or what.

"My aunt Bettina invited me to come stay with her for the weekend," she said excitedly. "There's some kind of spring festival going on. I haven't seen her in months—it should be fun."

I struggled to hold back my relieved exhale. "Oh, that does sound fun."

"You?" She tilted her head, looking at me.

I swallowed, giving a shrug. "Oh, not sure yet. Still trying to iron things out, but nothing concrete. Probably hang out around home some. Work on homework. Finish memorizing lines. You know, same old." I was babbling, a terrible sign, one that gave away I was hiding something.

Fortunately for me, she didn't seem to notice, just nodded thoughtfully. "So . . ." she drawled, staring fixedly at her hem. "How's it going with Jason?"

My heart thudded. I knew that was coming. "Not bad. Uh, practice is going well. We're working hard at blocking and memorizing. He's really good at it."

"Does he have his outfit yet?"

"I have no idea." I started stitching the lace to my sleeve. "We haven't talked about it or anything."

There was an awkward silence for several beats.

"Are you guys practicing a lot?" The words themselves were said lightly enough, but there was an undercurrent of an edge in her tone. This conversation was veering far too close to quicksand.

"As much as we have to," I said, trying to keep the irritation out of my voice. She was needling for information on something I thought we weren't going to discuss. Couldn't we have one day, one hour, go by where that tension wasn't there?

"What's wrong?" She put down her dress and eyed me. "Is there a problem discussing Jason?"

I put my sleeve down. "No, why would there be?"

"Is something going on?"

I bit my lip, took slow breaths to regulate my heart rate. "There isn't anything going on." Except a party I'm going to see him at on Friday night. And the almost-kiss. And our not-date date. So many secrets piling up.

And the biggest one of all—my feelings toward him.

Olivia raised her eyebrow. I could see one side of her jaw twitching, something she does when she gets frustrated. "If there's nothing going on, why are you dodging talking about him?"

I huffed a sigh. "I'm not trying to dodge it. I just don't want to talk about him for one day, okay?" Why couldn't she let it go? It was like she wanted me to confess everything I was feeling. But I was so not ready for that.

Things were far too unstable, too unsettled for me to even think about that as an option right now. I wasn't ready for the real possibility of Olivia blowing up at me.

"Fine," she finally said. But the stubborn set to her jaw told me it wasn't fine. And this was not going to go away anytime soon.

We sewed in silence for another twenty minutes or so, not talking, wrapped up in our own thoughts. My stomach was clenched so tightly it was a wonder I could breathe. I kept getting distracted, stabbing my finger with the needle. This lace was going to be spattered with blood if I didn't watch it.

I finished attaching the lace on the second sleeve then cleaned up the mess around me. "I need to go," I said. "I have a lot of homework to finish up." Not quite the truth—I'd done most of it before coming over. But I was tired of the awkwardness.

It had started out so nicely and went downhill so quickly. And all because of Jason. While I wanted to be frustrated and angry with him, it wasn't his fault. He had no idea how either of us felt about him.

She and I were in a silent competition with each other, Olivia trying to make me talk—and me trying to stay mum.

Things weren't going to last like this much longer.

Chapter ● Fifteen

I couldn't remember the last time I'd been so nervous.

I sat perched on the edge of the couch, heart racing so hard it was thundering in my ears. I eyed my outfit once more to make sure it didn't look too doofy. Black flats, jeans, a flowing sheer white shirt with a tank top underneath. Simple and hopefully not looking like I was trying too hard.

This was going to be a very different way to see Jason. I hadn't told him I was coming to the party, unsure how to broach the subject all this week. It might have looked like I was trying to flirt with him. Maybe he didn't even want to hang out with me—after all, most of our free time was spent together in play practice.

I wasn't sure I could face the rejection, so I simply kept silent.

The doorbell rang.

I jumped up and flung the door open. Lauretta grinned at me, her hair swept up in a messy ponytail. She looked adorable in high heels, ripped jeans, and a hot-pink shirt with skulls and hearts plastered across it.

"Omigod, you look fabulous!" she said, hugging me. "This party is going to be so much fun. Ready?"

I nodded. "As I'll ever be, I guess."

Mom darted out of the kitchen, eyeing me closely. Apparently I passed the inspection because she gave me a hug. "You two behave. No shenanigans. And you know what I mean."

"Mom," I said with a laugh, rolling my eyes. "Come on."

Lauretta crossed her fingers over her heart. "I swear to you, no shenanigans. Or tomfoolery, even."

She raised an eyebrow at me then Lauretta, but her face was relaxed. She loved Lauretta. "You two are trouble together, aren't you. Have fun and be home on time. *Don't* be late. And keep your phone on."

"It's all charged up," I said, suddenly antsy to go. I darted to the door. "Okay, bye, Mom!"

The drive there seemed to take forever. While Lauretta's older brother, Carlos, drove us to the house, Lauretta and I talked about everything going on in school this week—progress on the Renaissance faire, things we'd heard about who was dating and who'd broken up, and so on.

By tacit agreement, neither of us mentioned Jason. Now that she knew my feelings for him since I'd finally fessed up, she was maintaining a respectful space, letting me guide the conversation about him. But I knew if I wanted to talk, she'd listen.

It was a gift I gratefully appreciated.

I double-checked my purse to make sure the birthday card I'd gotten her cousin Jennifer was in there, with some money tucked inside. I'd never met her, but it seemed like a nice idea to not come empty-handed.

Carlos pulled into a cute neighborhood and drove another minute or two before parallel parking into a spot on the street. "Okay," he said, turning the car off. His grin was as wide as his sister's, and except for the scruffy dark-brown hair, he looked just like her. "We're here."

"Thanks for driving us," I said to him.

"You don't have to thank him," Lauretta whispered. "He's my brother. Mom made him drive me."

I laughed. "Still, doesn't hurt to be polite, right?"

Carlos gave me a smug smile, ignoring his sister. "And thank *you* for having manners."

My heart thrummed in my chest as we made our way down the street and to Jennifer's house. I could hear sounds of the band warming up out back, a guitar tuning up, drums and cymbals being pattered on. Luckily there weren't close neighbors nearby, with ample yard space nestled between each house, so no one would get bothered by the noise.

Carlos and Lauretta just walked right in, so I followed them into an open-floored living room and kitchen. It was nice and comfy, with plush couches and chairs set up everywhere. Teens milled around, laughing, drinking soda, and talking loudly. I recognized a few people from school too.

Wow, this place was packed. Jennifer must be one popular girl.

"I think the band's getting started," Lauretta said, leaning in close to my ear. "We should grab a drink, find Jennifer to say hi, then head back."

I nodded, suddenly nervous enough to want to put off seeing Jason for a few minutes. I needed some time to collect myself first.

We made our way into the kitchen, grabbing a couple of ice-cold soda cans from the fridge. Lauretta squealed and ran over to hug a tall blond girl.

"Jennifer!" she said. "You look fabulous. Happy birthday!"

I waved at her. "Hi, I'm Lauretta's friend," I said, fishing into my purse to give her my card. "Thanks for letting me come over!"

She beamed. "You didn't have to get me a card—that was so nice of you!" Apparently, niceness ran in the family. She was just as open and sweet as Lauretta. "You guys eat, drink, and enjoy. Have fun! We're having pizza delivered soon too, so I hope you're hungry."

After giving a parting wave, I made my way to the sliding glass doors, Lauretta right in front of me, clenching my free hand.

"Don't be nervous," she said quietly, peeking at me over her shoulder and giving my suddenly chilly fingers a big squeeze. "It'll be fine, promise. He'll be happy to see you, I'm sure."

I blinked. Wasn't sure why I was surprised she'd figured out the core of my fear, though—Lauretta was pretty intuitive. "Thanks," I whispered.

We headed outside, into the dark, warm air. Stars sparkled above us, and there were several large trees in the backyard providing an ambient environment. On the far left against the corner of the house was the band. I didn't know the lead guitar, but I recognized the drummer as someone from our school. I think he was a junior.

And there was Jason, wearing dark jeans, solid black boots, and a faded black T-shirt. The muscles in his arms stretched and moved as he did last-minute tweaks to tune his bass. His hair was mussed by the breeze, making him look much more casual and relaxed than usual. I swallowed.

That guy was the lead in our school play.

And I was going to be kissing him.

My heart rate picked up again, fluttering so fast I pressed a hand to my chest to soothe it.

The guys on the makeshift stage whispered to each other. Several girls lined up in front of them, bouncing on toes excitedly, giggling and staring at the musicians. I couldn't help but laugh at the sight. Didn't matter how famous the band was—there were always groupies.

The drummer clicked off the beat on his sticks, and they started to play. It was an upbeat song, one I'd never heard before—an original? How cool. I found myself being drawn closer to the band, Lauretta close at my side. We watched in silence, bopping our heads to the beat.

Jason stood off to the back, fingers plucking away at the bass. He looked natural up there. A real star. There was a crooked grin on his face as he bobbed his head to the music too, eyes just barely open. He was caught up in the music.

And I was totally caught up in him.

I exhaled a ragged breath. Wow, he could really play. He had a great ear for rhythm. I didn't know why he was so nervous talking to me about his music before. He was actually talented.

It would probably be fun a lot of to play a song with him sometime.

The lead singer moved up to the mic and began singing. The girls in front jumped up and down, squealing and dancing. Lauretta and I found ourselves doing the same, giving each other careless grins as we moved to the music.

The song was catchy, superfun. Just the right amount of clever lyrics to memorable lines. How had I never seen this band before?

The music went on for a good half hour. The band played a great mix of upbeat stuff, following up that first, original song with a string of covers. Jason was rocking his bass, eyes scanning the crowd. I was too far back for him to see me, which was good. It gave me a chance to relax and watch him perform.

"Thanks for listening! We're Eon, and we'll be back after a break." With that, the lead singer popped a CD into a sound system and hit PLAY. Dance music flooded the backyard, and the girls kept dancing.

I tugged on Lauretta's hand. "Let's move away before . . ." Before he saw us. I was still unsure how to approach Jason, especially after seeing the way the girls were gushing over the band right now during their break. I didn't need to look like a groupie.

Though I had to admit, I was starting to envy the attention they were getting. Jason walked over into a small group of girls and started talking. His hands were moving, his face animated as he spoke. Whatever he was discussing was something he felt passionately about.

One girl, a thin brunette, rested her hand on his upper arm and leaned in close. My stomach sank and I turned away.

"Wanna go freshen up our drinks?" Lauretta asked.

Relieved to escape the scene, I nodded.

We slipped back inside, me wrestling with my inner self. I had no right to feel jealous. He and I were nothing more than friends. Of course he could talk to anyone he wanted. I had no claim on him.

Though I longed for one, even if it was devastatingly apparent he didn't.

With a shaky hand I grabbed another soda. I wanted us to get closer. I wanted to drop all my guards and see if he liked me too. And if he did, I wanted to let this feeling grow into that one word I didn't dare let myself think, much less say.

"Oh!" Lauretta said after taking a sip of her drink, nodding toward the back corner of the living room. "I see some of my friends over there. Wanna go over and talk?"

"No, go on ahead," I told her. She was being supersweet, sticking by my side, but I didn't want to inhibit her fun. "I'm going to stand outside for a little bit and get some fresh air."

"You sure?"

"Absolutely." I waved her off with a stern look on my face. "Go now, young lady. Don't make me tell you twice."

She saluted. "Yes, ma'am." Bounding off to the living room, she squealed as she ran over and hugged a group of guys and girls.

I grinned and headed back outside. The band had dispersed, taking its groupies with it, and a softer song had come on. There were only a few people out here now. I walked over to one of the large trees and scooted down between its roots, breathing in the warm scents of grass and flowers. Jennifer's family had a small garden back here, and lilacs were blooming, perfuming the air.

"Nice and quiet back here, isn't it," a low, resonant voice said from just behind and above me.

I spun and looked up. It was Jason, smiling down at me. His face was backlit, the light from the moon and back of the house illuminating just the fringes of his hair and small parts of his nose, brow, and chin.

My heartbeat picked up and kicked into overdrive. "How did you know I was here?" I asked.

"I saw you. Tried to come talk to you after the set, but you'd already gone inside." He dropped down to sit by me. His warm cologne wafted over, mingling with the grass and flower scents.

He tried to find me? What did he want to talk about?

"I didn't know you were coming," he continued. "I saw you while I was playing. You should have told me."

I shrugged and said lightly, "Didn't need to feed your ego. You already have a bunch of girls clamoring for your attention."

He nudged me with his shoulder; heat permeated my upper arm from the contact. "But you're my biggest fan. I would have dedicated a song to you, you know."

I snorted a laugh. "Imagine how jealous my mom would be!"

"So . . ." His voice dropped down a bit. "Did you . . . did you like our music? We're still rehearsing and need to practice more, I know."

"Oh, it was great," I gushed, reaching out to pat his hand in comfort. Then I realized what I was doing—geez, I was touching him. Could I be any more forward?

I went to take my hand away, but he reached out and drew it closer into his.

"I'm glad you're here, Abbey," he whispered.

My pulse throbbed so hard in my body that I could barely hear him. All I could focus on was the softness of his breath, the way his thumb was stroking the inside of my palm. The earnestness of his words.

"I'm glad I'm here too," I said back.

"I want to know more about you." He lifted his free hand to

scrub the back of his neck. "I feel like you know a lot about me, but you're still a little mysterious."

"What do you want to know?" I couldn't believe I was making conversation with Jason. I couldn't believe we were sitting here under this tree, moonlight spilling around us, him holding my hand like it was the most natural, casual thing in the world.

And all I wanted to do was lean closer. It took every ounce of strength in me to stay where I was, to not give in and rest against his lean body. But I had to keep myself cool and focused. As best as possible, anyway.

"Okay. What is your favorite pastime? Other than violin and staring romantically at me during play practice," he added.

I rolled my eyes, glad for his joking. It helped ease me back into a comfortable space. "Um, when I get really bored, I play a lot of solitaire."

"That sounds so lonely," he said, voice rich with empathy. "We need to find you more friends."

"Hardy har. It's a great way to kill some time and be by myself. I know probably at least a dozen different solitaire card games."

"Wow, really?" This time he sounded impressed.

I nodded. "My favorite is killer solitaire. It's brutal—look it up sometime. What about you? How do you fill the time between all your adoring girl fans?"

"Well," he drawled, "there is so little time left after all of that."

I shoved against his shoulder.

"Kidding, kidding." He resumed caressing my hand, his

thumb making light swirls against the lower pad of my palm. "I like video games when I'm not practicing bass. Um, I also hang out with my brother—he's a handful, as you already know." He paused. "I guess I don't have anything else I really do consistently. You'll have to teach me some solitaire games."

I swallowed at the promise in his words. "I'd like that."

He looked at me, glancing at my mouth briefly. "I would too. Abbey—"

"Jason!" a deep voice said from the far end of the yard by the house. The lead singer, it seemed, from the tone. "It's time to start our second set."

He looked over at me, eyes filled with regret. "Can we pick this conversation up later?"

There wasn't anything I could do but nod.

He stood up, giving my hand one last brush before letting it go. With a smile and a nod, he headed back over to the makeshift stage, and I heard the tuning plucks of his bass a moment later.

I sat in place at the bottom of the tree for several minutes, pressing my hand to my heart. His cologne still lingered in the air, like he'd left part of himself behind. My stomach fluttered like it was filled with a dozen butterflies, clamoring to break free. I was bursting with life and a bunch of emotions deep in my core, ones that made me want to stand up and shout with happiness.

I couldn't deny what I was feeling any longer.

I was head over heels in love with Jason.

Chapter ● Sixteen

The rest of my weekend was spent in a glowing haze. After the band's next set at the birthday party on Friday night, Jason and I had talked for at least a couple of hours until it was time for me to go. I couldn't remember the last time I'd laughed so hard or felt so close to someone.

He told me stories about strange things his brother did and what he was like as a kid. He also told me about how his parents had almost gotten divorced last year but had worked it out. Now they were more in love than ever.

I told him about my older sister and our strained but slightly improving relationship. And about Don, who was a better father than my own biological dad, the man I barely saw because of his busy work schedule.

It was freeing and scary to delve so deep into myself and bare all. But he returned my trust with his own.

When we'd parted, he'd given me a full grin and told me he'd see me Monday. Of course, Saturday and Sunday dragged like crazy, in spite of my shopping trip to buy my required portion of Renaissance faire decor for our class decorating party next week. To help kill time, I even picked up extra chores around the house, something my mom could scarcely believe.

Monday morning finally arrived. I was keyed up with nervousness, excitement, fear. Would Olivia read my face and instantly know how I felt about Jason? I was sure I was glowing from the inside out, certain everyone in school would see. Luckily, she and I hadn't talked much over the past couple of days because of her being out of town, just exchanged a few generic text messages.

Somehow I managed to avoid her until our World History class. I slipped into my seat and gave her the biggest smile I could muster when she got in a minute later.

"Hey, did you have fun this weekend?" I asked brightly, fighting to keep my attention on her and not look around to see if Jason was in the room yet.

With a heavy sigh, she slid into her seat, slumped back. "Yes, but I am so drained! We did a lot of running around. It was fun, though. You?"

Jason walked in then; I saw him look at me and smile as he passed. My heart thudded, and I swallowed.

"Um, I did," I said, tearing my attention away from him and

back to Olivia. "Did some stuff around the house. Hung out with Lauretta. It was good. Fun. Lots of fun. But busy." My rambling was getting out of control. *Stop it!*

She quirked an eyebrow but didn't get a chance to respond because Mrs. Gregory came in right as the bell was ringing and clapped her hands, her thin metal bracelets jangling.

"Okay, class. Do you have your decor? All of the sophomores have been going down to the gym and working on their portion. It's our turn now. Gather your things so we can make our display and sale tables ready."

I grabbed my bag and stood, following the other students bearing bags out of the room, down the hall.

"What did you end up getting?" Olivia asked me. "I brought some small woven containers."

"Just some various things to help our table look festive. And I found these cute finger puppets I thought we could sell during the faire."

"That's perfect!" she said. "Kids will love it."

"I bought some face paint," Jason said, slipping right between us. "That'll be a lot of fun."

Olivia blinked, and her smile grew bigger as she eyed him. "Oh, hey! That's awesome—are you doing a face-painting booth?"

"Actually, I was assigned to be a floater and help others out. So after I get my booth set up, maybe I can work with you guys on your tables and the puppet show. If you want, that is."

"Of course we want," she declared.

I nodded dumbly. Any chance to spend more time with Jason was welcome . . . so long as I could keep from acting like a total idiot. And also tamp down these flare-ups of jealousy every time Olivia turned up the charm for him.

When we got to the gym, I nearly gasped in surprise. Several of the other classes had already been down to set up their tables and sections, and the large room's transformation into a real faire had already begun. Two of the walls were covered with large woven tapestries and blankets of bold tones and weaves, similar to what we'd seen in the art museum. There were arms and armor displayed in corners—not real, of course, since our principal wouldn't let us bring in genuine weapons—but the look was good enough to fool most people. Bright colors and ribbons were strewn up and down the rows of tables where our wares would be hocked.

A bubble of excitement welled in me. "This is going to be so cool," I whispered, bouncing lightly on the balls of my feet.

Mrs. Gregory guided us to our class's row, which was a line of undecorated tables. "Make it festive," she said loudly, her voice echoing off the walls. "We want people to be drawn to our goods. And make sure to help others if you have time! Participation is part of your grade, and I'm watching."

I nodded and got to work with Olivia on first setting up our table. We'd decided early on that we were going to sell our stuff together. We draped the table in a pale-green cloth and tied bows and ribbons along the trim. The work went fast.

"Ready to move to the puppet show area?" I asked her.

Olivia nodded. "My dad helped me make the stage and brought it in this morning. It's beside one of the bleachers." She looked around. "Hey, Jason!" she hollered. "Um, can you help me carry my puppet stage over to the far end of the room?"

The green-eyed monster peeked up in me again. I knew what she was doing and was irritated by her flirting. She wanted to play helpless. "I could help, you know," I said. "It's not that heavy."

"He's already on his way. Don't worry—Jason and I have this covered."

I swallowed back my irritation and focused on gathering my supplies to help decorate the miniature theater.

She and Jason maneuvered it into the designated area, off to the side near where Jason would be doing face painting. "Thank you so much," she gushed.

He smiled. "No problem. Um, you guys need any more help?"

"We totally do." She tapped her chin with her forefinger. "How about you start with decorating the front, and I'll add the curtains. Abbey, can you work on the sides?"

"Sure," I said flatly.

She didn't notice my tone or ignored it, gathering fabric in her arms and draping it across the front of the large hole where the puppet show would happen.

"What time did you end up getting home on Friday?" Jason asked me.

Olivia stopped in place, her back stiffening.

I swallowed, heart thudding painfully. Crap. I was so busted. "Um, not too late. It was a fun party—Lauretta said Jennifer gushed about how great you guys played." I tried to play up the angle of him being in the band and lessen our personal interaction, despite my desire to talk more to him.

"There was a party?" Olivia asked. Her voice was light, but I could see something in her eyes.

Jason nodded, grabbing some fabric and material to staple along the front of the minitheater. "Yeah, our band played for a birthday party."

"Lauretta's cousin Jennifer," I added. "There were a lot of people there. Too bad you were out of town."

"Yeah. Too bad." This time her voice was the one that was flat, and in it was tinged a warning. I would definitely be hearing about this later when Jason wasn't around.

Guilt mingled with anxiety and frustration. I didn't owe her any explanation, did I? I was at a public party, not a private date with Jason.

"What if we do a few stripes of this color and this one"— Jason held up red and yellow fabrics toward me—"on the front and sides? Do you think that would work? The colors might look good against the curtains."

At least he wasn't picking up on the tension between us, despite the feeling it was all about to boil over. "Yeah, that would be great."

We cut several strips, working in silence and tacking them

on the wood as Olivia crafted her curtains in a rich green velvet.

"So, you play in a band?" Olivia asked. "What's your instrument?"

"Bass." Jason squinted and stuck out his tongue just slightly as he stapled a strip into place. It was adorable. "But I have a long way to go before I'm as good as Abbey. She's a natural."

In spite of the frostiness radiating from Olivia, I melted just a little bit from the kindness in his words. "I'm still learning too. And I thought you guys sounded great. Um, your whole band worked hard, I could tell. The audience loved you guys," I added.

"I'd love to hear you play sometime," Olivia told him softly.

"Not sure when our next gig is, but I'll let you know." The words were said nicely enough, but the meaning was clear—he wasn't planning on playing any special gigs just for her. Why? Was it because he didn't like her?

Could it be because he liked me?

The phantom feelings of his fingers in my hand on Friday night made me clench it into a fist.

Olivia was quiet for several more minutes. She finished draping the green curtain the way she wanted it. Jason and I got our fabric in place as well.

"Thanks for your help," she told Jason. There was a strange formality in the statement. Something had changed in the air—I think Olivia knew something was up. And I'm sure the hot flush burning my cheeks didn't help things. "And you, too, Abbey. I'm glad to see you've got my back."

With that, she balled up the scrap fabric in a bag and walked away.

Practice was going terribly.

"I . . . crud, hold on," I said, fumbling in my pocket for my script. I'd forgotten my lines yet again.

Jason stood there, unusually silent and patient. I knew he could tell things were off but didn't prod me to talk about it.

And that was good, because what was I going to say? That my best friend knew something was up with us and hadn't talked to me since yesterday during the decorating—no texts, no in-class notes, nothing? It wasn't Jason's fault that he'd become a "thing" between us. I couldn't drag him into it.

Added to that was the stress that it was our last solo practice. The faire was next week, and neither of us had time to meet alone before then. We had only two more group practices, as well.

Between all of that, I was stressed, flubbing my lines, forgetting what I was supposed to say and where I was supposed to stand. I couldn't focus. I just wanted to sit down and have a good cry to get it out of my system.

"You seem . . . off," Jason finally said. "What's wrong?"

I huffed a sigh. "Just stressed. That's all."

His brow furrowed and he moved closer. "Seems like more than just stress. Wanna talk about it?"

"Jason," Braedon said from his seat a few rows back, "my green crayon broke. Can you fix it?"

He shot me a regretful glance. "Hold that thought." Then he hopped down off the stage to help his brother, who was busy coloring a picture to keep himself occupied while we practiced.

I sat down on the edge of the stage, feet dangling, heels thunking the front panel. How had things gotten so crazy so fast? Would Olivia stay mad at me forever? Should I just talk to her and tell her how I was feeling, what was going on?

Was there anything going on?

And was I going to be this scatterbrained during the play? Lines were escaping me quicker than I could believe. Panic swelled. Frustration thundered at the sides of my temples.

Argh! I wanted to pull my hair out. This was getting to be too much.

I swallowed and jumped down, going to my bag. "I should go," I said. Suddenly I had an urge to get out of there, to go stand outside and get some fresh air, clear my head a bit. I needed perspective.

"What? Wait, hold on," Jason said. He turned to Braedon and whispered something then rushed down the aisle over to me, pulling me to a seat in the front row. "Sit. Talk. Something's up, and we need to get it out, now."

Reluctantly I did as he said and took a steadying breath. "I'm . . . I'm kinda freaking out. The play is next week, and I'm forgetting lines left and right. What happens if I screw it up? Everyone's worked so hard." I blinked back a sudden stab of tears.

I was not going to cry about this—not here. "Um, sorry . . ." I glanced away.

"Hey, it's okay," he said gently, tilting my head back toward him. His eyes were soft and understanding. "This is normal. You have the jitters. It'll go away once we get out there and perform."

The stuff with Olivia wasn't going to go away, and I couldn't talk to him about that or about my feelings for him. But maybe he was right. Maybe once I got onstage, the rest would come together. I could only hope. "You think so?"

"Absolutely. I'm there with you. We'll get through this together." He dropped his hand and placed it over my own. A gesture of comfort, yet it heated me and made my heart race madly.

"Have you ever freaked out before?" I asked.

He laughed. "Are you kidding? I was so scared on Friday night before that gig that I thought I was going to throw up. I didn't eat for hours beforehand."

My eyebrows shot up. "What? You looked like a natural. So smooth and—" I stopped myself from saying handsome, biting my lip to keep that word inside.

"And what?"

I cleared my throat, glanced away. "Um, you looked great."

Fortunately, he let that slide. "You are a natural at this, Abbey. Mr. Ferrell picked you because no one else could play this role like you can." The words were gentle but insistent. "Now, let's get back to practicing. It's our last chance to rehearse alone, and I don't want to waste it. Okay?"

I took his hand and we went back on the stage, glad he was taking control of the situation. It helped ease some of the tension in my stomach.

"Okay, let's start from the top of Act Two." His eyes bore into mine. "You know these lines. Don't force it—just let it happen."

I took a moment to breathe in, out, then nodded. I could do this. He was right. I'd get through practice and then talk to Olivia tonight, try to clear the air. Surely, she'd appreciate me trying to be considerate of her feelings.

And if she didn't . . . well, I couldn't think about that right now. One step at a time.

"I'm ready," I told him. "Let's do this."

Chapter ● Seventeen

I love your dress," Lauretta gushed on Tuesday, the morning of the Renaissance faire. Shoving her pale pink sleeves up, she reached toward my head. "Let me fix a few of those braids though, okay?"

I braced my hands against the porcelain sink of our school bathroom and nodded. "I couldn't reach the back very well, so I think some of them are crooked. And when I tried to twist them, well . . . you see what happened."

As Lauretta braided and twisted, creating perfectly elegant hair, I eyed myself in the mirror, nervous beyond belief. My gown hugged my top nicely, flaring just under my bodice into an elegant drape that shimmered even in the dingy bathroom light. My makeup was light; the nearly permanent flush on my cheeks made blush unnecessary. I hadn't even risked trying to put on eyeliner with as much as my hand had been shaking.

Fortunately, the play wasn't until tomorrow evening. I could make it until then.

If only things weren't so awful between me and Olivia.

"So, where's your partner in crime?" Lauretta asked, once again pretty much reading my mind.

I sighed, taking a tube of lipstick out of my small purse and puckering my lips to apply the soft, nearly nude color. "I don't know. She hasn't talked to me since early last week." Several days had passed now with no response to my texts or calls. I'd tried to reach out to her, but she didn't want to be reached.

Things were going to be so awkward at our booth. My butterflies kicked into overdrive, making my stomach flutter even more.

"She knows how you feel about him, huh?"

I kept my head still and met her eyes in the mirror. "I didn't get a chance to even explain my side of things. She put two and two together, basically." Like it had been hard, though. I could barely keep my mind off Jason; no wonder my emotions bled through onto my face.

"She'll come around." Lauretta did a few small tugs on my hair, adjusted some of the pins. "There. Sheer perfection."

I took out my compact mirror and eyed the 'do. So much better—she'd made me look casually elegant, twisting the braids into a braid of their own and pinning them to my head. "Thank you so much." I put the mirror and lipstick back in my purse. "Do you need help with anything? Though you look perfect," I added.

She grinned. "Nah, I'm good." Her smile slipped a little. "But I'm worried about you. You don't seem like yourself. I know this stuff with Olivia is taking a toll on you, but try to not worry, okay?"

I gave her a hug, careful to avoid our hair from entangling. "Seriously, you rock. Thank you for being there for me." My throat closed up. Lauretta had always given me so much care and attention. It was a balm for my poor heart right now. "I don't know how I'd get through this without you."

She pulled back and grinned. "You'd do horribly, I'm sure. Just kidding—you're stronger than you know. Now, buck up, kid," she said in a deep, manly voice, chucking me on the chin. "We have a Renaissance faire to attend. You ready?"

I sucked in a breath and nodded.

We headed out of the bathroom together and made our way down the hall toward the gym. Music greeted us long before we got to the doors, along with laughter and the buzzing of lots of voices.

When we opened the doors, both of us gasped. We hadn't seen the gym since our classes had done our portion of decorating. Now, with the decor fully done, it felt like we were plunged into an historical, genuine faire. I couldn't fight the smile on my face; the environment perked me up instantly.

"Welcome to ye olde town faire," a sophomore guy I didn't know said from right beside me, clad in a Harlequin outfit with bold, colorful tights and tunic. He thrust a program into my hand. "This here flier tells ye where ye can find any goods ye wish for."

I curtsied. "I thank ye," I replied, slipping into my role. I turned to Lauretta. "Come, dear, we must head into the festivities."

She grinned. "But of course!"

We took our time going to our booths, winding up and down the crowded aisles. Practically the entire school was there, all classes milling about, talking loudly overtop of each other. The tables were packed with all kinds of craft items, books, and the like. It was almost overwhelming.

Lauretta stopped at her table and squeezed my hand. "Okay, I have to do some time here, but I'll drop by and see you soon."

My heart raced as I walked to my table. Olivia was already there, dressed in her beautiful green gown. Her eyes met mine, and she glanced away.

"Hi," I said quietly.

She nodded.

"You haven't been returning my calls. We need to talk about everything. Please don't ignore me." I tried to keep my tone level so as not to sound accusatory, though it hurt my feelings that she could brush me off like that.

"I'm not ignoring you," she said stiffly. "I've been busy getting last-minute stuff ready for the faire."

I knew she was lying, but what good would it do to call her out on it? "Okay. Maybe we can talk later then."

"Yeah, sure." A customer came over, one of the adults who was browsing up and down the aisle, and she pasted on a fake smile. "Good morrow, sir! Can I interest you in any of these fine wares?"

I let her be, scanning the crowd to see who was in attendance. I recognized a lot of upperclassmen. They all seemed impressed by the costumes and music—a wandering group of minstrels stopped and serenaded females as they passed, and the girls blushed and giggled in return.

Clever. I couldn't help but chuckle a little.

Then I saw Jason. He was a couple of aisles down, sitting in front of a little girl who had her cheek bared to him. A slender brush in his hand, he dipped the tip into a small pot of paint and applied it to her face. Her eyes were bright, filled with excitement.

My heart squeezed. Maybe he'd paint something on my cheek—that could be fun. Would it make Olivia upset? Impulsively, I wanted to grab her hand and have us go over there together, but that might make things worse.

I sighed, dropping my attention down to the various goods scattered across our table.

"Abbey," my mom said, stopping right in front of me. She was grinning from ear to ear. "This is awesome!" Leaning in, she whispered, "And don't tell your sister, but I think it's even better decorated than her faire was."

"Thanks, Mom," I said, giving her a grateful smile. "Um, are you interested in buying anything? All of the proceeds are going to help our school."

She raised one eyebrow. "Yes, I remember that from last time. And of course I'm going to buy something." She glanced over at Olivia. "Hey, long time, no see. Where have you been hiding?"

"Hi, Mrs. Wilks," Olivia said, studiously not looking at me. "I've been busy with school stuff."

"Ah, I see." Mom looked at me, a little bit of pity in her eyes. She handed me some money then picked up a few small wicker items. "Okay, I'm going to browse some more. You girls have fun. And you both look lovely, by the way."

Olivia and I both mumbled our thanks as Mom walked off.

Wow. This was getting more awkward by the minute. The strain and tension thickened with each passing moment of silence between us. I pursed my lips. I'd had enough—I needed a break.

"I'm going to look around and get something to drink," I said.

Her face tilted away, she waved me off in a dismissive manner. "I'm on rotation to do the first showing of my puppet play after I help sell some food, so be back in a half hour or no one will be here manning our table."

I nodded stiffly and walked into the thick of the faire, looking for the booth selling drinks. I found one four rows over, the table laden with some kind of punch.

"Greetings!" a guy in thick glasses announced from behind

the table, waving his hand toward the cups. His shirt was a bright purple striped with red. Didn't exactly scream authenticity, but I guess it wasn't my place to critique his costume. "We have the finest ale in the land."

"Nonalcoholic, I assume," Jason said from right beside me, popping up out of nowhere.

I jumped, pressing a hand to my chest. "You have to stop sneaking up on me like that," I replied with a laugh.

He eyed my costume for one long moment then swept into a deep bow. "Milady, you look enchanting."

I bit my lip, curtsying. "Milord, your clothing is simply perfect." His breeches looked like they were real leather, molding to him as if they'd been handcrafted for his form. His white shirt had puffy sleeves, which he'd slitted and added ribbons of color underneath. The outfit was topped with a black velvet vest, buttoned to his throat.

It was as if he'd stepped out of the pages of a history book. Together, we looked like we could slip into a royal court.

"Are either of you thirsty?" the guy behind the table asked, interrupting my admiration of Jason.

We both turned our attention to him.

"Uh, sorry," I said, flushing.

Jason held up two fingers. "And these are on me," he said before I could reply, digging into his pants and fishing out money.

I accepted the drink with slightly shaking hands. "Thank you." A sip showed it was actually a tasty punch, with hints of fruity sherbet.

We walked over to Jason's table, where a few kids waited impatiently for him. "Finally, you're back," a little boy with curly black hair proclaimed. "I want a tiger on my face."

A woman behind him, who I assumed was his mom, nudged him in the shoulder with a frown.

The boy glanced up at her then back at Jason, mumbling, "Please."

Jason laughed. "Sure thing." He settled into his seat, taking the brush and getting it ready.

"Um, do you need any help?" I asked. "I have a little bit of time before I need to go back to my table."

"Really?" He grinned, his eyes warm. I melted just a tiny bit. "I'd love it. There's an extra chair behind me—pick up a brush and help yourself."

I perched on the end of the chair and waved over the next person in line, a little girl who was no more than four or five. She had on a princess crown with a veil streaming behind her thick curls. "Hi, sweetheart," I said to her gently. "What would you like me to paint on your cheek?"

She pursed her lips, deep in thought. "Um, a butterfly?"

"Butterflies are beautiful," I told her solemnly. "Good plan. What are your favorite colors?"

"Um"—she glanced up at her dad, who gave her a smile and nod of encouragement—"I like red and blue. And orange."

Eclectic. I liked that.

I could feel Jason glancing over at me as I stroked the color across her chubby face. It took all of my efforts to focus on her and not gaze back at him. I made flashes of her favorite colors in the butterfly tails, making the body of the butterfly a rich blue. I topped it off with black antennae then reached over to grab a mirror Jason had laid out.

She took it in her fumbling hands, peering intently at the butterfly. "It's pretty," she declared without moving that side of her face. Smart girl—wanted to let the paint dry so it wouldn't get smeared or marred. "Thank you."

"You're welcome," I said and took the mirror back.

"Daddy, I'm hungry," she said as they walked away. "And I want a dress like that girl's. It was pretty."

Jason and I exchanged grins. It was intimate and fun, sharing this activity together with him. I was glad I'd gotten away from my booth for a bit.

The next twenty minutes or so went far too fast. With regret, I retired the paintbrush and wiped it clean. "I need to man the booth while Olivia does her puppet play," I said.

"Hey, when are you eating?" he asked. Was I imagining things, or was there a light flush to his cheeks?

I swallowed hard, my own cheeks burning in response. "Probably around eleven thirty or so. You?"

"The same. Would you . . . do you want to eat together? I checked out the array of food, and there are some potpies that look good."

"Yes, sure, absolutely," I gushed.

"Okay, see you back here then?" He dotted dabs of paint on a girl's face.

I nodded and turned to go.

"Abbey," he said.

I turned back.

"You look beautiful."

I was pretty sure I floated all the way back to my table.

Chapter Eighteen

I stood at the table for a good hour, trying to look upbeat and answer questions about our goods. A couple of people strolled by, perusing, picking stuff up and then dropping it back down. I ended up spending a lot of time fixing and straightening the baskets because of it.

A small crowd was forming near Olivia's play. She'd asked me to stay at the table, but I really wanted to see her skit. A part of me hoped that maybe if I went over and supported her, cheering and clapping loudly, she'd stop being upset with me. She'd see how hard I was trying, and we could talk things out.

When a few more minutes passed without any shoppers, I impulsively grabbed all of our stuff and swept it into a bag, shoving it under the table. After the show, I'd come back and sell more.

Doing a walk-run, I darted over to the puppet stage. Olivia

must have finished decorating it last week; it looked professional with all the trimmings. I made a mental note to tell her so.

There was a group of kids in front of me, standing restlessly and squirming. They were obviously eager for the show to start.

The stage's curtains parted, and a puppet was thrust up into the hole. "Welcome to the puppet show," Olivia said, her voice slightly muffled from her hidden position in the large wooden box.

The kids clapped, and a couple of boys whistled loudly.

But even that didn't add luster to Olivia's voice. It was lifeless as she brought the other puppet up and said, "This is Rosalyn and William. William's brother loves Rosalyn, and they're supposed to be together, but she secretly loves William, and he loves her. So the brother ends up alone."

My face burned, both with anger and embarrassment. How dare she drag our personal issues into this? Could she behave any more childishly right now, be more obvious?

The kids stopped moving, fixing each other with confused stares. I couldn't blame them. This show was growing worse by the minute. Olivia wasn't even bothering to read the lines, just having them talk to each other about how much they were in love.

After ten minutes, all but one kid had left. I was struggling to keep my anger under control. It was painfully apparent Olivia felt she was wronged, that Jason and I were mean to her. Well, she was wronging me here—not even giving me a chance to talk.

She assumed she knew everything going on . . . that there was something between me and Jason. He hadn't even told me how he felt, if he felt anything at all.

"Oh, William," the female puppet said in a simpering tone. "I'm unable to resist you, in spite of my previous promises to another."

This was just getting ridiculous now. I stomped off to the food area, chest tight and fists clenched. How could she be so selfish and so self-centered? So much for being best friends. Instead, she was choosing the passive-aggressive route, taking all her frustrations out on me with puppets.

The backs of my eyes burned; I blinked away the tears. I wasn't going to cry over her. Not now.

I wiped a hand across my eyes, trying to not smear my makeup, and walked resolutely to the food area. There was a turkey leg booth, with a few of my classmates waving and shouting the prices. Jason was supposed to meet me here soon. I didn't want him to see me upset.

I sat down at one of the open tables, swallowing several times and breathing slowly through my nose. Anger wasn't going to help anything right now. It was clear that Olivia was going to make this a deal breaker for our friendship.

But beneath my anger was a big layer of guilt and hurt. She and I had never fought like this before. Then again, I'd never liked someone she did.

A couple walked by, fingers threaded together as they whispered in each other's ears. Jealousy pinched me in the stomach, and I sighed. Would I ever have that with Jason, even if it permanently drove Olivia and me apart?

And did it make me a bad person if I did?

Speak of the devil, Jason strode up to me, a crooked smirk on his face. "I was going to try to scare you like I always do, but you were facing me this time." He got closer, and a frown marred his brow. "Hey, you okay?"

I straightened in my seat. "Fine, thanks."

He sat down across from me. "You don't look fine. Your eyes are puffy and—"

"I'm fine," I insisted. There was no way I could talk to him about this. In spite of my anger with Olivia, I wasn't about to admit how she felt about him, or how it had driven a big wedge between us.

He closed his mouth, his eyes shuttering just slightly. "Fine. Are you hungry? Do you still want to eat?"

I bit my lip. Had I hurt his feelings, shutting him out? Why did it seem like I was screwing up everything lately? "Yeah," I said with a forceful smile, "I've been eyeballing those turkey legs for the last few minutes."

He nodded, but that casual easiness from earlier seemed to be gone. "Okay, I'll go pick some up for us."

I dug into a small pocket sewn in my dress and handed him a few bills. "This should cover both of us."

"I don't need money." His jaw was set tight.

"You bought our drinks. I can buy the food," I insisted, thrusting the money closer to him.

"Why? It's not like this is a date, is it?" he threw back.

Ouch. My heart slammed against my chest in a furious beat. I stood. "I'll just go buy my own. Thanks."

"No, wait," he said, grabbing my hand. "Sorry, that came out wrong. I'm . . ." He ran his hand across his face then scrubbed it through his hair, mussing the top. "Can we talk for a moment? Before we eat?"

I gave him a tentative nod, and we sat back in our seats.

"Jason!" Beth, a junior said, walking up to him with a big smile. "Your outfit looks amazing. I can tell you put a lot of effort into it. If you'd been in our class last year, our faire would have been even better." Beth planted a hand on one slender hip and beamed down at him, her red hair glowing softly in the gym lights.

Geez, even older girls liked Jason. I put my hands in my lap, struggling to maintain a neutral face.

He smiled. "Thanks, Beth. We all put a lot of work into our faire. You should drop by my table later, and I'll paint something on your face."

Was he flirting, or just being polite?

Her smile grew bigger. "I will, thanks. See ya later." She finally looked at me. "Oh hey, Abbey. Pretty dress."

"What did you want to talk about?" I asked him after she finally left.

Jason sighed, gaze skittering across the slightly thinner crowds. "I'm not quite sure this is the right place. Sorry, I'm just . . . I'm stressing a little. Must be the play giving me nerves."

For a moment, I'd sworn he was going to talk about us. Good thing I wasn't the betting type or I'd have lost that gamble. "You're going to be amazing," I said, making myself sound more upbeat than I felt. "Remember what you told me? Just be confident in yourself."

He turned to look at me, his eyes so serious and intense that I couldn't look away. "Abbey, do you want to talk about anything? Is there something on your mind?"

"Oh no, I'm fine," I said quickly, the lie rolling off my tongue with ease. "Really." I smiled. "Let's get something to eat, okay?"

"Okay, but—Hey, there's Olivia," he said, looking just past my shoulder. He smiled and gave a small wave, then frowned for a quick moment. "She looks mad. Wonder what's wrong?"

"Probably just ticked off about her show," I said, trying to keep the emotion out of my voice. "I don't think it went really well."

"Oh." He was silent. Then he stood, giving me a polite smile and offering his arm. "Well, let's go grab something to eat before the lines get too long."

I managed to avoid Olivia for another couple of hours. After eating, I went back to our table and reset it up. She stayed away, making her way from booth to booth, helping others out. Her avoidance was so obvious there was no way for me to ignore it. She didn't want to see me and didn't want to talk to me.

Guilt ate away at the fringes of my conscience, warring with resentment.

By the time school ended, I'd had enough. This wasn't going to work—I refused to let her ignore me. I'd made sure to pack up our table early, keeping a close eye on her to see where she went when the bell rang.

Olivia wove her way through the crowd, me secretly just a few feet behind, pushing through people and apologizing for my rudeness several times. I received a few glares, but no one got in my way.

As the crowd surged toward the exits, Olivia split off and went down a side hallway, practically running. I kept on my toes and followed her.

She darted into a nearby bathroom, the door almost slamming shut behind her. I stopped it with my hand and forced it open.

"What—" she said, spinning around. Her eyes narrowed when she saw it was me. "Abbey? What do you want?"

I backed up against the door, pinning her in the room. "Out with it," I said. "No more running from me."

She crossed her arms, leaning one hip against a sink. "Out with what?"

"Olivia, I saw your play. And I know you're mad at me. Stop pretending like you're not." Frustration made my voice shake.

She pursed her lips, huffed out a sigh, which blew strands of her hair away from her face. "Fine. You want the truth? I hate that you lied to me about how you feel about Jason. You knew I liked him, but you still went after him."

"That's not—"

She held up a hand, her face devoid of emotion. I'd never seen her this upset, to the point where she was completely cold. Even her voice was icy. "I don't even want to hear it. You snuck and went to a party just to see him, which I had to find out about later. From *him*, of all people. Don't try to tell me you're not hiding things from me. How could you?"

"I swear, that's not how it was. I couldn't stand him at first—you know that. And when I realized . . ." I swallowed. No backing out now. "When I realized I liked him, I tried to fight it. Because I know how much you do! And I didn't want to hurt you."

"Well, you did." Her eyes slitted more, but in the corners I could see a shimmer of tears. The coldness was gone in a flash, replaced by a bitter hurt. "You upset me worse than anyone else could have, because you were my best friend, and you knew how I felt about him."

I dropped my attention to the floor, guilt surging so heavy I couldn't bear to look at her pained face anymore. "I'm sorry," I choked out through a closed throat. "If I could stop myself from liking him, I would. I fought it for a long time. But it's not as though he likes me back, you know."

Her scoff made me raise my head. One eyebrow was lifted

as she studied me in scorn. "You're kidding, right? I've seen the way he looks at you. He's never looked at me like that before—or anyone else, for that matter."

Instead of giving me hope, her words made my guilt stronger. "It's not true," I whispered hotly. "He doesn't like me, and nothing's ever going to come of it."

"You know what? I don't even care," she yelled, waving her hand dismissively. "It doesn't matter if anything ever comes of it. The point is, you knew how I felt about Jason, and you didn't care. You still chased after him. Best friends don't do that to each other, Abbey."

"I didn't chase him," I retorted, my voice raising until I was hollering too. "You're mad and exaggerating things. That's not how things happened at all, but you refuse to listen to reason. It's easier for you to be mad at me."

"You two go be a happy couple. Let him be your best friend. The two of you deserve each other." Olivia pushed past me, ripping the door open and flinging it wide, stomping into the hall.

I stayed in the bathroom for at least fifteen minutes, not fighting the hot tears sliding down my cheeks.

Chapter ● Nineteen

My stomach wouldn't stop churning. I stared blindly at the mirror in the small dressing room, patting on my makeup.

Since my fight with Olivia after school yesterday, I'd been in a haze, walking home by myself, closing myself off in my room and only coming out for dinner. And today's faire had been even more awkward than yesterday's, with she and I working solo shifts, not looking at each other the entire day.

Jason, obviously sensing the tension, stayed away for the most part except for a quick check to make sure I was ready for today's performance. Even that was stilted, though—my continued silence on what was bothering me made things less warm and connected between us. More like we were at the start of rehearsals.

Olivia's angry words kept echoing in my head nonstop, despite my best efforts to drive them out. She was wrong about me.

But also right.

And that made me even more frustrated. How could I fix this? Did I even want to anymore? My best friend, my confidant, threw me aside because I dared to like someone she did. It was selfish of her.

Yet if she'd done it to me, I'd have been hurt too. I would have felt selfishly upset. Because of the magnitude of my feelings for Jason, I could kind of understand and empathize with her pain. If it turned out he liked her, not me, my heart would break into a hundred pieces.

Some of the cast members buzzed and flitted around the room, a cacophony of whisperings about makeup and costumes and the play swirling in the air. I finished dabbing on my lipstick and stood, doing one last look-over to make sure I was presentable and ready. It was time to shake this funk off—I didn't want to be miserable or let this drown me in sorrow. I'd deal with it later.

For now, I had a performance to do. If I could rise above my personal issues and let myself become fully entrenched in my role, this would prove to me that I could really make it in the arts. All the great actors, musicians, and performers had to.

One of the minor cast members patted my shoulder. "Break a leg!" she said excitedly, her grin practically splitting her face in two. Her hair was pulled back in a white wimple, and her gown was understated in a muted brown but still eye-catching. "This is going to be great."

I let her enthusiasm wash over me, giving her back the biggest smile I could make. "You too, thanks."

Jason walked in, dressed in his garb and makeup already on, still looking as handsome as he did yesterday. He saw me and nodded, walking over with his face neutral. "Hey, you ready?"

I knew it was my fault things had gotten strained and funky with us, but for a moment I wished I could simply spill everything on my mind and make it better. He'd turned out to be not only an incredible guy but also a good friend. Not being able to talk to him was torture. But out of some deep-seated respect for Olivia, I couldn't. "Yeah, I think so. You?"

He nodded.

I missed his teasing. My mind scrambled for something we could joke about, but before I could come up with anything, Mr. Ferrell came into the dressing room. Everyone stood and faced him, and Jason lined up beside me, his fresh cologne wafting to my nose.

Mr. Ferrell was dressed in period garb as well, his peach-colored shirt made of a thick linen, paired with dark-brown pants and leather sandals. Several of the girls sighed in unison upon seeing him. Couldn't blame them—he was really handsome. "Hello, cast!" he said, excitement pouring into his voice, his eyes twinkling. "You've worked so hard for this moment."

A few cheers broke out.

"When you're out there, live your role one hundred percent. Let everything else go—be in the moment and love it. You've got this down. I've watched practices, and I know you guys can do it."

I let his words buoy my spirits. He was right. I could do this, could let myself shake off this dispirited funk and enjoy the moment.

"Curtain's up in ten minutes. Finish getting ready, and break a leg!" Mr. Ferrell gave one last parting smile then swept out of the room, leaving us in a frantic race to help each other finish dressing, putting on makeup, and securing hair, props, and everything else.

The lights blinked off and on. It was time.

My stomach suddenly pitched in a rush of nerves. I gathered up my skirts and quietly made my way to the back of the stage, peeking around the curtain. The entire school was there for the play, along with parents and others. It was a packed house.

I swallowed.

A hand brushed my arm. I turned to see Liana, dressed in her gown and smiling at me. "You're going to do great," she whispered. "You have this role down pat—it was practically made for you."

I blinked in surprise. "Um, thanks," I said, feeling a little guilty at how uncharitable I had been toward her. Yeah, she'd flirted with Jason, but could I really blame her for that? He was everything a girl could want in a guy. "I learned a lot by watching your practices," I added.

She squeezed my arm then slipped away to the other side of the stage, joining the rest of the nonspeaking cast who would be milling about when the play started.

The curtain went up, the house lights dimmed, and the spotlights shone on the stage. The play had officially begun.

By intermission time, I was coated in a slick layer of sweat. In spite of our full dress rehearsals, I hadn't realized how hot I would get, probably inflamed even more by my edgy nervousness. Jason, however, had only a few dots on his brow. How he managed to look so cool and collected was beyond me.

He'd flirted with me like a man falling in love throughout our scenes, pulling me into a web so deep I couldn't help but find myself tumbling for him deeper. He was William, and I was Rosalyn, and I was swooning over him in spite of myself.

What an echo of my reality.

I took a swig of my bottled water, glad for a brief break. After intermission, some of the secondary characters would be onstage for a good chunk of time without me, and I could grab a quick stretch out the back door, maybe get fresh air for a few precious minutes. The dress was clinging to my skin from all the sweat, and I desperately needed a breather.

When the house lights flickered off then on, I took the opportunity to delve deeper behind stage, winding my way through the narrow black hall and slipping outside. Instantly I was greeted by the balmy evening air. The sun was cresting over the horizon, sending splashes of reds, pinks, and oranges streaking in the west.

The sweat on my skin instantly dried, and I sighed in sweet relief.

Just up ahead of me, I could see the dark silhouettes of a couple of guys—closer scrutiny showed it was Jason and another member of the cast, talking in hushed tones. A part of me itched to sneak closer to see if I could hear what they were talking about, but that would be wrong.

I made myself stay in place, leaning carefully against the warm bricks of the school wall as I studied Jason's profile, so familiar to me now that I could draw it in my sleep. He let out a low chuckle, the sound resonating across my skin.

I loved him.

I loved him, and I was pushing him away because I couldn't tell him my feelings. It was ridiculous. But what could I do? I'd already hurt Olivia. If I confessed, who was to say he'd feel the same way?

I drew one last long breath then went back inside. We were nearing the end of our play, the pinnacle scene where I was supposed to let him kiss me.

Would he even still want to?

A horrible thought struck me—was it possible Olivia was out in the audience? Likely not. Odds were, she was too bitter and angry with me to even dream of supporting me. But if we kissed onstage, it would be the final nail in the coffin.

How could I do that to her?

I pressed a fluttering hand to my uneasy stomach. And how could I kiss him, my first real kiss, knowing that would open the floodgates to my feelings, ones I'd been so desperately keeping inside?

I wasn't ready for this. To be laid open bare before him, before the entire school. He'd know I was in love with him.

Mr. Ferrell came up to me, ever-present clipboard in hand. "Okay, your last scene's coming up soon. Go get 'em, tiger. Make it one wallop of a kiss—but school-appropriate, of course," he added with a crooked grin.

I gave a weak nod, moving backstage and swigging down the rest of my water, my mouth suddenly dry.

Then it was time for me to go back onstage for the climactic ending. Somehow I managed to fake my way through it, in spite of the horrendous twisting nervousness of my stomach. My eyes were practically drawn to Jason's mouth, wondering what it would feel like on mine. Then I'd mentally smack myself to look away and stop thinking about it.

Would we kiss?

Jason strode toward me, his face bearing none of the earlier indifference he'd had in the dressing room. No, it was open and warm and inviting. A fine acting job, one that twisted my heart. I wanted it to be real.

"Rosalyn . . ." He drew me to center stage, as we'd practiced. The lights were hot as they focused on us, brightened in intensity. "I can't live without you. I . . . I love you."

In that moment, I knew I needed to hear him say it for real. And the probability of that happening was next to nothing.

With a bittersweetness tingeing my words, I pressed a hand to my chest. I turned my face from him, not wanting him to see that genuine rawness in my eyes. It was hard to force the gaiety in my response to him. "Wait, you . . . you love me? But how can this be? You have done nothing but tease and torture me from childhood on. Our whole history is built upon this strange antagonism between us."

Jason clenched my hand tighter. Instead of laughing, as he normally did at this part, he was strangely silent, his tone much more serious and sincere than I'd expected. "From the first time I pulled your hair at the side of the river," he said, the words almost inaudible above the slamming of my heart against my rib cage, "I knew I loved you. How could I not? Especially when you returned my attention with a punch in the nose—well deserved, I might add."

I moved away from him, blinking a couple of times. "I never knew you felt that way. Why did you not speak of these feelings before . . . before your brother made his intentions clear toward me?"

Jason took my hand, turning me toward him. His grip on my fingers was warm, and I thought there might have even been a little bit of a tremble in them. But that couldn't be, right? "Would you have trusted me, had you known?" He shook his head. "I have railed against this for far too long, believe me. My heart did struggle with the knowledge that I could not let my brother win your hand. Not when . . . when I wanted it for my own. I could no longer remain silent."

I stepped closer to him until there was barely a breath separating us. Our lips were just a few inches apart. I was transfixed by his eyes, losing myself in the moment, the strength of his hands in mine, the tingle spreading across my skin. "Oh, my dear William, I love you too."

Jason leaned toward me, eyes growing heavy-lidded then closing.

I closed my eyes too.

And I saw Olivia's hurt face.

With a regretful sigh, I turned until his lips brushed against the edge of my cheek instead of my mouth, wrapping my arms around him to pretend like we were kissing. It was horrible, and I was flooded with instant regret and sadness.

How badly I wanted to kiss him. But I couldn't do it, not like this.

We pulled apart, and his eyes were so sheltered I couldn't read his face at all. Then he stepped away, pasted on a huge, bright smile, and faced the audience. It looked like there was a tinge of relief in his features.

Applause broke out and rippled through the audience, along with whistles. The rest of the cast flooded the stage, stepping in front of me and Jason, who had moved several inches away. His absence was painful, and I shivered.

I had fooled myself. Jason didn't want to kiss me. He was obviously all too happy we hadn't.

He and I took our bows, the applause cresting.

Then I turned and walked offstage, trying to pretend like my heart wasn't cracking apart.

Chapter ● Twenty

That was amazing!" my mom said, thrusting a dozen red roses at me when I finally stepped out of the greenroom, back in my regular clothes and face scrubbed clean of the last vestiges of makeup.

"You were great," Don added, hugging me with a tight squeeze. "I've never seen you act like that, kiddo. You have talent."

"Thanks," I told them, cradling the flowers in my arm. Their rich aroma filled my senses but didn't offer any relief from my sadness. To my horror, tears began stinging the corners of my eyes. I pretended to lean down and smell the roses, using the opportunity to furtively wipe the wetness away.

"Your sister was talking to some of her friends but she'll be— Oh look, here she is," Mom said as Caroline darted her way over and hugged me.

"That was incredible," Caroline breathed. She pulled back, and her eyes flicked a brief moment of concern before she schooled her features into a smooth, gentle smile. "Hey, let's get you out of here. I have a feeling you probably just want to unwind in your room or something."

I gave her a grateful nod. We walked home, Mom and Don talking almost nonstop about how professional the production was, how much they enjoyed the dialogue and found the play fun. I inserted nonverbal "uh-huhs" and "yups" where needed, but my poor mind wouldn't stop replaying that stage non-kiss.

The strangeness in Jason's eyes afterward, and then what looked like relief as he pulled away from me. I hadn't imagined that.

What kind of a fool was I? To lose my best friend over someone I'd fallen for yet was now in no better of a spot than her when it came to winning his love. The worst kind of fool. One who was left alone.

Ugh, my maudlin attitude was even starting to frustrate me. This was getting beyond ridiculous. I shifted the flowers in my arm. I needed a mental break from myself, from my stress. I needed to do something artistic that didn't involve anyone else.

I glanced at my sister, who was nodding and talking with Mom and Don. They'd moved on to talking about the whole Renaissance faire, gushing about how fun and interesting it had been.

"Hey, Caroline," I said tentatively. "Um, do you think you'd be able to take me up to the park? The . . . well, I think I want to practice my night shots, and it's the perfect evening for it."

Mom frowned. "It's getting late, honey. How about you do that tomorrow after school, since you don't have play practice anymore?"

"I don't mind staying with her," Caroline offered, giving me a small smile. "And we won't stay out late."

Relief hit me fast and hard. She could tell I needed to get away from everyone and clear my head. "Yeah, I promise," I said, crossing my heart.

Mom pursed her lips and looked like she was going to say no, but Don squeezed her shoulder, giving her some kind of a knowing look. Mom sighed. "Fine, but don't stay out late, ladies. You have school tomorrow."

Like I needed the reminder. It was going to be doubly awkward. Dread spiraled in my body in anticipation.

I'd deal with it tomorrow, though. For now, I just wanted to relax and let go.

We made it to the house. I darted inside, put my flowers in water, then grabbed my camera and stood by the car, waiting for Caroline.

She slipped outside a minute later, dangling the car keys in her hand. Her grin grew wide. "I could tell you needed to escape," she said with a small laugh. "I've had that same look on my own face on more than one occasion. Mom means well, but sometimes she doesn't know when to back off."

"Thank you," I said, briefly squeezing her hand.

We slipped in the car, and she turned on a rock station but kept the volume low. My gratitude for her grew as I realized she wasn't going to press me to talk. I'd never fully realized how cool Caroline actually was. Naturally, I'd revered her when we were little. But as I'd gotten older and she'd hung out with her friends, ignoring me, I'd grown to feel disdainful, the gap between us widening.

Yet here we were, in comfortable silence, her whisking me off to the park without asking any questions or demanding any information.

That was a balm to my battered heart.

She pulled into the parking lot in front of the sprawling stretch of the park's bright-green grass and shut off the car. With a little twist she turned to look at me. "I can tell you need some alone time. I'm going to stay in the car, but if you want to talk, I'm here." Her eyes were so warm and open, I almost started crying.

I nodded and gave a watery smile, opening the door and going outside. The park only had a few people milling around, a couple of teenagers swinging on the swing set and laughing. The sky was wide and open here, the fringe of trees far off and the lights dim enough that I could see specks of stars.

Even the air itself was calm. I smiled and let it soothe me.

From a tree stump, I propped my camera up and tweaked the settings for night shots, playing around with shutter speed and such until it was just right. Then I sat down on the grass.

This would have been fun to share with Jason.

A smile cracked my face when I remembered taking pictures of him playing golf. He really did have a lot of talent. Sure, he wasn't a photographer, but I'd bet if he was given a camera, he'd figure it out fast and become an expert. He was driven to succeed, to thrive at whatever he took on.

I heard a soft giggle and turned my head. There were two teens still on the swing set, holding hands as they rocked back and forth and whispering to each other. The girl's eyes glowed with love. The guy's responding smile was easy and genuine.

I sighed and recalled the feel of Jason's hand in mine at the party. How hard I'd fooled myself into thinking I had a chance with him. I'd made the actor's classic mistake and gotten caught up in the romance of our practices, forgetting the reality of our situations, our lives.

My camera finished its sky shot, and I grabbed it, snapping a few frames of the couple, zooming in on their faces and making the background blurry. Even without seeing them on my computer, I could tell the shots were going to be good.

After doing another half-dozen shots of the park, the lights casting an eerie glow on the trees, I put my camera away and headed back to Caroline. She was perched on the front of the car, laughing into her cell phone.

When she saw me, she quickly said bye and hung up. "Did you get whatever you were looking for?"

What a loaded question. Did I?

Taking pictures of that couple had filled me with a bittersweet longing. I'd tried to escape into my art but couldn't. At least, not today.

Still, I nodded, not wanting her to feel like'd she wasted her time bringing me here. "I got some good pictures. Thanks again."

With a quick squeeze, Caroline hugged me then headed to the driver's side, me popping into the passenger's seat. "I told you before," she said as she turned the car on. "If you need to talk, I'm here. I may not have the answers, but I can listen."

We headed home, music playing softly as we sat in companionable silence.

I gave my sister a grateful smile. In spite of my romantic flop and destroyed friendship, something good came out of this situation. Caroline and my relationship had shifted; we were on more equal footing now. Somehow I knew that she'd have my back, should I need it. And I'd have hers.

Despite that comfort, it was still well into the night before I was able to finally fall asleep.

At lunch on Wednesday, I sat at the table, finishing the last few bites of my peanut-butter-and jelly-sandwich. There were a couple of junior girls at the other end, talking loudly and punctuating the air with chortles and hand gestures as they told some sort of story.

"And then I totally told him he looked completely ridiculous," the brunette said, holding her stomach as she laughed. "Those pants were far too tight. But Devon didn't care. He just strutted down the hallway—well, more like an awkward shuffle."

I snorted, taking a drink of my soda.

A tap on my shoulder drew my attention to my left. I turned, and there was Olivia, peering down at me. Her eyes were a little puffy underneath, with dark circles makeup couldn't quite hide.

After not talking to her since Monday's blowout, I was surprised to see her. I took a steadying breath. "Hey."

"Hey," she replied, glancing at the still-gabbing girls then at me. "Um, do you have time to talk?"

My heart started pounding, my hands shaking slightly from nervousness. Olivia didn't sound or look angry anymore. Around her there was an air of solemnity, tinged with a bit of sadness. "Yeah, sure." I stood, grabbing my soda and trash. A tiny flame of hope flared up in me, but I was too afraid to let it grow.

"I thought we could go to the library," she said as I pitched my trash.

In silence, we strolled into the library, taking a table far from anyone else. There were a few guys looking through books, but they ignored us. I tried to keep my face neutral yet open as we settled into our seats.

What did Olivia want to say to me? Yeah, she didn't seem angry anymore, but that didn't necessarily mean this was going to be a good conversation.

Olivia planted her hands on the table, fingers twisting around each other. She swallowed, touched her hair, swallowed again. Her nervousness, oddly enough, eased up a little bit of mine. I kept my hands in my lap, pressed hard to my thighs, waiting for her to start.

"So, I've been thinking about everything the last couple of days. You, me, *him*, all this stuff going on," she began. "It's crazy how complicated and dramatic everything turned."

I nodded.

"And . . . I know that was partly my fault. Okay, more than just partly." She sucked in a deep breath, fixing her intense stare on me. "Abbey, I was so mad at you. You knew I really liked Jason." I opened my mouth to speak, but she held up a hand. "No, wait, please let me finish."

I bit back the defensive words that had been on my tongue. "Okay."

"I was mad for a few different reasons. Jason was always . . ." She tilted her head to the side, gaze drifting off as she stared blindly at the shelves behind me. A wistful smile spread on her face. "He was the 'ungettable get,' you know? The one guy who was an unattainable dream to me. There's something unreal about him, the way he draws people in."

She was right about that. I nodded in agreement.

"So there was no harm in my silly crush because deep down, I knew nothing would ever come of it." She stared down at the names carved into the surface of the table. "And even though I was upset you didn't like him, I was secretly glad. Because that meant he could be all mine."

"I never meant to hurt you," I said then bit my lower lip.

"Olivia, if I could have stopped the way I felt about him, I would have. It's been . . ." I sighed, letting my words stall out. It didn't matter anymore, anyway.

Olivia looked up at me, and there was a sheen of tears in her eyes. "I was wrong to be so mad at you. You can't help the way you feel about him. And I know you fought it. You did because you knew it would upset me." She paused. "But I was so filled with self-righteous anger that I wasn't able to see that. Until the play."

I blinked. So she'd been there. That meant she'd seen the non-kiss. "I didn't know," I said. "Given . . . everything going on, I figured you'd have stayed away."

Her eyes filled with knowing. "You had a moment up there, at the end. I could tell you were supposed to kiss him, but you turned your head. And my gut told me you'd done that out of loyalty to me." Her voice broke on the last couple of words. "But I'd thrown that friendship away, and I regretted it."

I reached over, not bothering to fight the tears in my eyes, and squeezed her hand. "I hate that this came between us," I whispered.

"I don't want to fight with you anymore." She sniffled, a tear rolling down her left cheek. "And I don't want to get in the way of you two being together. I want you to be happy."

My own tears burst forth as my heart squeezed tightly. "There is no us. I . . . I misread the situation. I got caught up in the acting and thought he might actually like me, but he doesn't."

During gym this morning, Jason hadn't even looked at me,

much less tried to talk to me. It was clear that now that the play was over, things were going back to the way they were before. Us as strangers.

She frowned. "No, that doesn't seem right. He definitely likes you."

I shook my head. I didn't want to get into it or bring her down when we were repairing our relationship. "It doesn't matter," I said, waving my hand. "What's done is done, and school will be over soon enough."

Then there would be a whole summer of no Jason. No reason to even see him. The thought left a hole in me.

"Have you told him how you feel?" Olivia asked.

I scoffed. "And how would I do that?"

She rolled her eyes. "'Dear Jason, I'm madly in love with you. Love, Abbey.'"

I gave a genuine chuckle. "You make it sound so easy."

"It *is* easy."

"He's just . . . he's been so hot and cold that I don't know how he really feels." So many mixed signals. But that last one knocked me for a loop . . . and sent a distinct message. "I can't put myself out there like that. Because if he told me he didn't like me, it would—" I stopped, but Olivia knew. It would crush me.

And I wasn't ready to hear it from him.

"So you're going to just let him go because you're too scared?" She shook her head in disbelief. "This is so unlike you."

"Well, I've never fallen for anyone before," I retorted.

"Do you regret it?"

Did I? In spite of the way things had gone, there was something utterly captivating about this feeling of falling in love. A passion I'd never known existed and wouldn't have if it weren't for him.

How could I wish that away? It enriched my life, made me see things through new eyes. Yeah, I'd never have Jason, but I'd always have my feelings. And that had to count for something.

"No," I answered honestly.

The bell rang. We gathered our stuff and made our way out. Before we reached the door, Olivia pulled me into a tight hug.

"Let's never fight like this again," she said, her voice almost hoarse with emotion. "These last couple of weeks have been awful."

I squeezed her close. "Never," I swore.

"I still think you should tell him," she added as she pulled away, guilt flaring up in her eyes. "He should know how you feel."

We headed to the hallway, slipping into the crowd. "I'll think about it," I said, mostly to pacify her and ease her remorse.

With a parting smile, Olivia shuffled off in one direction, and I went in another, glad to have made up with her but unable to lessen the other source of discomfort.

Jason.

Chapter ☕ Twenty-One

A bbey," a deep voice called from behind me.

I turned, squinting at the bright sun as Jason wove through the students exiting school for the day and came toward me, backpack slung over his shoulder. Instantly my heart began beating a rapid staccato.

I remained frozen in place. His eyes were hooded, unreadable, his mouth pressed into a thin line. He looked irritated, taking long strides toward me like a man on a mission. Had I done something to upset him?

He hadn't said a word to me in World History, keeping his attention firmly on the teacher the entire class period. And when the bell had rang, he'd grabbed his stuff and run out of class like the room was on fire.

"You and I need to talk," he said point-blank once he reached me. "Do you have time right now?"

My stomach sank. I nodded. While I was happy to have resolved the issues with Olivia, it had drained me. I wasn't sure I was ready for round two with Jason. But he looked frustrated and obviously needed to talk.

Maybe I could apologize for whatever I'd done. I opened my mouth to start saying I was sorry, but he blurted out, "What's with you lately? Why are you blowing hot and cold with me? Did I do something to make you mad?"

I blinked, frozen in place. I hadn't anticipated him being so assertive, but that was Jason. Then his words sank in. A slight tremble ran across my skin. "Wait, *me* blowing hot and cold?" He was the unreadable one, not me.

He tugged me by the elbow over to the edge of the sidewalk to let a large group of girls pass by. When they were out of hearing range, he said, "Yes. You've totally pulled away and are shutting me out. I thought we were friends. But friends don't treat each other like this."

A burst of disappointment exploded in me. *Friends.* That was all we'd been this whole time, and nothing more. I was stupid to think I'd seen any chemistry in his eyes toward me. Obviously I'd misread everything.

Idiot! I cursed myself.

I jerked my elbow out of his hand. "Yes, we're friends. Nothing has changed. I'm just . . . going through stuff right now."

Suddenly I wanted to run away, to escape the piercing stare of his eyes. Everything I wanted to tell him was surging to the front of my mouth, desperate to spill out, and I couldn't do it. I couldn't be vulnerable to him right now.

"What stuff do you mean? And why have you been brushing me off lately and not talking? And what was with . . ." He cleared his throat, his cheeks burning a bright red. "What was with that kiss during the play?"

Tell him. Tell him. The chant echoed in my brain, but my body trembled with vivid fear of the consequences of the truth. "I couldn't hurt my friend's feelings," I said, hedging a bit.

He blinked, confusion flooding his face and making him squint at me. "Why would our acting hurt someone else?"

"Because Olivia has a crush on you, okay?" I said more forcefully than I meant to. I quieted my tone. "And if she saw—" I stopped, horrified at where that sentence was going to lead.

"If she saw what?" he pressed, stepping closer to me. His warm breath puffed a few tendrils of hair. His eyes were wide, insistent, unflinching. "Why would it be bad for her to see us, Abbey? Tell me."

My throat closed up. I looked down, staring at his feet. "If she saw us kiss, she'd know . . . that I, I like you. And you'd know too, because I wouldn't be able to keep it in anymore. And I didn't want you to know, but now I've dug this hole so deep and messed up—"

Suddenly my face was tilted up, and Jason's mouth was on

mine. Warm tingles instantly spread from my lips throughout my body as he kissed me.

He was kissing me!

I was so shocked for a second that I just stood there. Then I melted against him, wrapped my arms around his shoulders, tugging him closer, needing to feel him. He draped his arms around my waist, our bodies curved close. He was strong and lean, his mouth gentle, unforceful as we kissed. My heartbeat slammed throughout my limbs, roared in my ears.

Finally he pulled away, pressing his forehead to mine. "I have wanted to do that for so long," he whispered.

"Really?" I couldn't fight the smile on my face. "But why . . . why didn't you ever tell me?"

He chuckled. "Because you hated me, remember? And I realized once we started our play practice what a jerk I'd been for judging you. I thought you'd never like me, and that I'd killed any hope of you wanting to date me."

"Well, you were a big jerk," I teased.

He lifted his head to give me a mock glare. "You didn't make things easy on me either. You are a very hard person to read."

Me, hard to read? Here I'd felt like I'd worn every emotion on my face, petrified he was going to figure it out. A thought stopped me. "But . . . why did you look so relieved after we didn't kiss onstage?"

He furrowed his brow. "Huh? That wasn't relief at us not kissing. It was relief that I'd be able to go escape and try to gather my thoughts, to figure out how I'd screwed things up." He paused. "It hurt my feelings that you'd rejected me."

He'd seen it as rejection. A hot flush of guilt burned my cheeks. No wonder he'd pulled away—he'd misread the situation completely.

The way I'd misread him.

"I'm sorry," I whispered, stroking his arm. "I wasn't rejecting you. But . . . my friend would have seen us kiss, and I was afraid of hurting her. I knew if we did that she'd see my feelings."

"And what exactly are your feelings?" His eyes were so penetrating as he stared at me.

My flush grew stronger. He liked me, but I *loved* him. Deeply, passionately, stronger than I ever could have imagined. Maybe I could downplay my feelings and take it slow. And maybe one day, he might feel the same. . . .

He reached one hand up to stroke my cheek, keeping the other firmly pressed on my back. "I love you, Abbey."

I gasped in a shallow breath.

"I've loved you and have struggled with how to show you. Even Braedon could tell—he hasn't stopped teasing me about it since he saw our last practice."

At that, I giggled. "Really?"

His face sobered a bit, and a multitude of emotions flickered across his eyes. "Do you think . . . well—"

"I love you too," I interrupted with a soft whisper, wrapping my arms around his waist and pulling him into a hug. I didn't want him to doubt it, or me, anymore. No more secrets. No more confusion.

Just real, true honesty.

I felt the moment he relaxed, pulling me deeper into an embrace. He rested his chin on the top of my head then pressed a kiss to my brow.

"Abbey, I want you to be my girlfriend."

I looked up at him. His eyes were shining, open. All that emotion had been there the whole time but I hadn't seen it. Was too afraid to trust in my instincts. But I wasn't doubting it now. Jason loved me, loved being with me. And he wanted me to be his girlfriend. "I'd love to," I said, then paused. "But one thing."

"What's that?" He frowned.

"You can't make me golf with you," I said solemnly. "Because I stink at it and I'm never going to be as good as you."

He huffed out a laugh, wrapping an arm around my shoulders as we moved back down the sidewalk. "You drive a hard bargain."

"And I also want you to write me a song," I continued, warming up to our easy, teasing relationship. He was going to keep me on my toes, so I'd better keep him on his. "And maybe—"

"Abbey," he interrupted, stopping again in place and staring down at me.

"What?"

"Stop talking." Then he pressed his mouth to mine, slipping his fingers through my hair and caressing my neck.

I sank into his kiss and, for once, I was all too happy to comply.

TURN THE PAGE FOR MORE FLIRTY FUN.

I t started as just another normal Sunday afternoon. I was wiping down tables at College Avenue Eats. That was normal. My family had owned the place for three generations, and I worked there part-time after school and on weekends.

We were between the end of brunch and the start of the dinner rush, so the place was pretty quiet. There were a couple of university students at the little round tables by the big front window, heads bent over their laptops. An old guy at the counter was nursing a cup of coffee and reading the local paper. Still normal.

My best friend, Simone Amrou, was in the corner booth cramming for tomorrow's biology test. *Definitely* normal. "Opposites attract" was a perfectly sound scientific principle (magnetism, anyone?), but even if it wasn't, I would have believed it based on my lifelong friendship with Simone.

Exhibit A? I'd started studying for the test the same day Mr. Ba announced it two weeks earlier. Simone? Not so much.

"Help me, Bailey!" she wailed as I straightened the salt and pepper shakers on the next table. She widened her puppy-dog brown eyes and stared at me soulfully. That generally worked on guys, especially paired with her exotic good looks. On me? Nuh-uh.

"I told you to read the chapters as we went along." I flicked a stray cupcake crumb off a chair with my rag. "Then you wouldn't have to cram at the last minute."

"I know, Miss Logic, I know." Simone sighed, poufing out her already-full lips to blow a strand of wavy dark hair out of her face. "But I was busy with that English paper all last week, and then Matt wanted to hang out at the park yesterday—"

"Bailey!"

This time it was my cousin calling me from behind the counter. Susannah was nineteen, four years older than me, and a sophomore at the university.

"Be right back," I told Simone. When I reached the counter, Susannah was staring at the cash register with a peevish expression on her round, pretty face. "What's wrong?" I asked. "Did Methuselah die again?"

That was what we called the ancient cash register, which had been around since my great-grandparents started the business. My family was nothing if not consistent.

"Not this time, thank goodness." Susannah smiled, making deep dimples appear on both cheeks. "Do you know where your mom put the register tapes? I can't find them, and she just left to pick up your sister at gymnastics. I can call her, but you know she never picks up when she's driving, and—"

"No, it's okay. I'll find them." I hurried through the swinging saloon-style doors leading into the kitchen. My dad and Uncle Rick—Susannah's father—were just coming in from the delivery bay out back, both of them lugging tubs of donut glaze.

"Can you get the door, Bailey?" Dad grunted as he hoisted his tubs onto the big marble-topped island where Mom and Great-Aunt Ellen rolled out the pastry for the bakery business and the bread for the deli stuff.

I kicked the door shut, then grabbed one of the tubs my uncle was juggling and set it on the stainless-steel counter along the wall. "Suz can't find the register tapes," I said. "Has Mom been reorganizing again?"

My dad traded an amused look with Uncle Rick, who was Mom's brother. "Always," Dad said. "Check the blue cabinet. I think she put the office supplies in there this time."

"Thanks." I headed for the supply room. Everyone in the family knew Mom loved to reorganize. The problem was, she usually moved everything around and then forgot to tell anyone else where she put it all.

When I passed through the kitchen again, Dad was stowing

the last of the tubs under the counter, and Uncle Rick was on the phone.

"Three dozen mixed sandwiches for a week from Saturday?" He jotted something on a pad. "Got it. Will that be delivery or pickup?"

"Spring Thing order?" I asked Dad quietly. The Spring Thing was an annual event at the university—three days of fun, special events, and goofiness to celebrate spring before the crunch of finals set in.

"Guess so." He rubbed his bald spot the way he always did when he was distracted. "Can't believe how many orders we've got already. Gonna be a busy weekend."

"That's good, right? The more orders we get, the more money we make."

He grinned and tousled my chin-length brown hair as if I were still eight years old. "That's my girl," he said. "Always the math whiz!"

"Funny." I smacked his hand away with a laugh, then headed out front with the register tape.

Susannah was on a stool behind the deli case, hunched over a thick textbook. The page it was open to had tons of tiny text and no pictures at all.

"Got a test coming up?" I asked.

"Always." Susannah wrinkled her nose and glared at the book. "Tell me again why I decided to major in business administration? This stuff just doesn't make any sense!"

The little brass bell over the door jingled. A man I vaguely recognized as one of the English professors at the university came in.

Susannah watched as the professor paused to scan the specials board. "Is Deena back from break yet?" she asked me. "Looks like I'm about to have a sandwich order. And the evening crowd will start trickling in pretty soon."

"Don't think so, but our dads are both back there." I flipped open Methuselah's case, which gave way with a creak, and quickly changed out the tape. "They can make a sandwich if they have to."

As Susannah greeted the customer, I headed over to see how Simone was doing. She grabbed my arm and dragged me down onto the seat beside her. "You have to help me, Bails!" She sounded desperate. "I'm so going to flunk tomorrow!"

I glanced at the table. Her textbook was covered in Post-it notes, and other random bits of paper were scattered everywhere. "Okay, where are you stuck?"

"Everywhere," she moaned. "Starting with, what's the difference between DNA and RNA again?"

I sighed. Sadly, this too was normal.

"Okay, so they're both nucleic acids, right?" I said.

She looked blank. "Right?"

"Simone! Didn't you do *any* of the reading?" This was bad even for her. Mr. Ba's class was tough, and he didn't tolerate slackers. It was an accelerated class, and he expected his students to be serious about learning. I loved that. It made me feel like I was already in college learning real stuff instead of marking time in high school.

"I *read* it." Simone stuck her lower lip out in that cute little pout that drove boys crazy. "I just didn't *understand* it. We can't all be science geniuses like you, Myers."

The bell jingled again as another customer came in. I glanced over automatically. I didn't recognize him, which definitely *wasn't* normal, since he was a guy about my own age. There was only one high school in our town, and it was small enough for everyone to know everyone else, by face if not necessarily by name.

Simone spotted the new arrival too. "Who's *that*?" she hissed, elbowing me hard in the ribs.

"Ow! I don't know." I rubbed my ribs and sneaked another look at the guy. He was in line behind the professor, checking out the stuff in the bakery display case while he waited. Kind of tall. Dark brown hair that curled at the temples and the back of his neck. A nose that was a little long and slopey in a way that made his whole face more interesting.

"Maybe he goes to that Catholic school out by the mall," Simone whispered. "Oh! Or he could be a senior from out of town who's touring the campus."

"He doesn't look old enough to be a senior." I shot her a sly look. "But it's a good thing if he's from out of town. You're going out with Matt now, remember? And this guy looks like just the type to tempt you—you know, tall, dark, and handsome."

She tore her gaze away from the guy just long enough to raise one perfectly groomed eyebrow at me. "Yeah, he is pretty cute. It's not like *you* to notice that, though, Bails."

"What? I have eyes." I quickly busied myself straightening her mess of papers. "So back to DNA versus RNA . . ."

"That can wait. Come on, let's go say hi." Simone shoved me out of the booth so energetically I almost hit the floor. I recovered with a less-than-graceful lurch and a grab at the nearest table. Tossing a look toward the counter, I was relieved to see that the guy had his back to me.

"Wait," I hissed. "What are you going to say to him?"

Simone ignored me, grabbing my hand and dragging me along. With my free hand, I quickly smoothed down my hair as best I could. How much had Dad messed it up just now?

And more to the point, what difference did it make? As soon as Mr. Tall Dark and Handsome got a look at Simone, he wouldn't spare a glance for my hair if it was on fire. That was life, and I was used to it. Kind of liked it, actually—it saved me from a lot of embarrassment and stress. Because while I had no trouble chatting with other girls or adults, I was notoriously tongue-tied around guys my own age. I just never seemed to know what to say when faced with that Y chromosome. I was pretty sure it was some kind of syndrome. Maybe I could do a study on it after med school.

Simone, however, was not similarly afflicted. "Hi, there!" she said brightly, tapping the guy on the shoulder. "I'm Simone, and this is my friend Bailey. Are you new in town?"

The guy looked startled, but then he smiled. "Is it that obvious?"

Simone let out her giddiest, most charming laugh. "Only because this is, like, the smallest town in the universe. Right, Bails?"

"Uh?" I said. "I mean, yeah. Except for the university. If you include the student body, I mean, it's actually quite . . . But that's not, you know . . ."

Okay, yes, I was floundering. Obviously. Luckily, Simone came to the rescue. "So are you here for a campus tour, or what?" she asked the guy.

"Not exactly." He looked even cuter when he smiled. "My family just moved here. Actually, we're in the middle of moving in right now—that's why my parents sent me out to pick up some food." He gestured vaguely at the deli counter. "Our new kitchen's kind of a mess."

"You came to the right place," Simone told him. "Eats has the best food in town—just ask Bailey. Her family has run it for like the past million years."

"Really? Cool." The guy turned and studied my face. His eyes were very blue. I held my breath. What was I supposed to do now? My mind was a vacuum. Not as in vacuum cleaner. As in the scientific term for a complete absence of matter or substance.

This time it was Susannah who came to my rescue. "Can I help you?" she called out as the professor moved out of the way, clutching a steaming cup of coffee.

"Yeah, thanks." Mr. Blue Eyes stepped forward. "I need to order some sandwiches to go. . . ."

As he started to give his order, I yanked Simone away. "We should get back to studying."

"Are you mental? We can't abandon your hot new friend." She poked me in the side, making me squawk. "Didn't you see how he was looking at you? And he's obviously smart, too. Just your type."

"What? No. What do you—shut up." I frowned at her.

The loud *cha-ching!* of Methuselah's cash drawer distracted me. I glanced over just as Susannah said "Okay, that'll be about five, ten minutes."

"Thanks." The guy barely had time to turn and face us again before Simone reached out and tugged lightly on the sleeve of his T-shirt.

"MIT, huh?" she said. "That just happens to be Bailey's dream school."

I blinked, noticing his shirt for the first time. It was gray with the red MIT logo emblazoned across the chest. How had I missed that? Or wait—had my subconscious mind somehow picked up on it without telling the rest of me? Maybe that explained why my attention was drawn to this guy with the strength of a neodymium magnet.

"Yeah, both my parents went there," the guy said. "By the way, I'm Logan. Logan Morse."

"Like Morse code?" I blurted out.

See? Hopeless at talking to guys.

Logan laughed. "No relation, as far as I know."

"So Logan," Simone said. "Why'd your family move here?"

"My mom just landed a tenure-track job at the university. Physics. She's really psyched about it."

"Physics? Your mom's a scientist?" I said, interested enough to forget my discomfort for a second.

"Bailey's a scientist too," Simone piped up. "Our bio teacher says she'll probably win the Nobel Prize someday."

I shot her a murderous look. Mr. Ba *so* hadn't said that.

"Really? Cool." Logan gave me another of those appraising blue-eyed looks.

"Um . . ." As I was figuring out whether it was actually scientifically possible to die of embarrassment, three or four people burst into Eats, laughing and talking loudly. College rugby players, I guessed, based on their clothes and the mud covering every inch of them from hair to cleats. Eats was a favorite stop after sports practices thanks to our Belly Buster specials.

"Suz!" one of the rugby players shouted. "Feed us, woman!"

Susannah rolled her eyes and smiled at the player and his friends, then glanced at me. "Think I'm going to need a little help back here, Bailey," she said.

"I've got it!" Simone exclaimed before I could answer. "I'll go make sandwiches. You stay right here, Bails."

I opened my mouth to protest, but it was too late. She was already scooting behind the counter. Simone worked at Eats part-time in the summer, so Susannah just nodded as she pushed past, heading for the kitchen.

As the rugby players clustered around the register, Logan and I stepped back. "This seems like a cool place," he said. "So your family has owned it for a long time, huh?"

"Ages. Since before my mom was born, actually." I was glad he seemed to be ignoring Simone's ridiculous Nobel Prize comment. Still, I couldn't resist turning the topic back to science. "So your mom's a physics prof? And she went to MIT?"

"Yeah. She and Dad met there as undergrads. He's a science guy too—paleontology. He's been working on a book while Mom climbs her way up the academic ranks."

"Works her way up?" I was distracted by the way his lips went a little bit crooked when he smiled, though I wasn't sure why. I didn't usually notice stuff like that about random strangers unless I was doing research for a human-genetics project or something.

"Yeah," he said. "First she was finishing up her PhD; then she had a bunch of nontenured jobs and stuff. So we've lived in a bunch of different places."

"Really? Like where?"

Logan leaned against an empty table. "We just moved here from Switzerland. Before that was Boston—we were only there for a year—and then Tokyo and California. We also spent a couple of summers in Botswana for Dad's research. And one in Singapore for Mom's."

"Wow." I wondered what it would be like to live that way—moving to a new city or country every couple of years.

"So what about you?" Logan asked. "Have you always lived here?"

"Uh-huh." I shrugged. "Totally boring, right?"

"Oh, I don't know." He flashed me that off-kilter smile. "There's something kind of nice about knowing where you belong. Maybe I'll finally find out what that's like. It looks like this time my family might actually stay put for a while."

"Oh." I'd observed Simone talking to guys for long enough to know that she'd probably have a flirty comeback for a comment like that. Me? Not so much. For a moment I'd almost forgotten I was talking to a guy. Now it all came crashing back, and Logan and I stood there staring at each other for what felt like forever but was probably only a few seconds.

"So," he said at last, "what's the local high school like? I'm starting there tomorrow, and I could use any tips you can give me."

"It's okay, I guess." I tried to think of something witty to say but came up empty. "Um, just a typical high school."

The door flew open again. This time at least half a dozen more rugby players poured in. At the same time, Susannah hit the little silver bell by the register.

"Morse!" she called out. "Order's up!"

"That's me." Logan glanced over. "I should get going, I guess. Looks like things are getting busy."

"Yeah. They probably need me to help back there." I stepped aside as a rugby player barreled past, shouting something about a bacon craving.

"Okay." Logan hesitated, shooting another look in Susannah's direction, then turning back to me. "I'll see you at school tomorrow, right, Bailey? You and—um, your friend."

I blinked. Had my ears deceived me, or had this cute guy actually remembered my name—and forgotten Simone's? That had never happened before.

"Yeah," I said just as Susannah shouted my name, sounding frazzled.

"Guess you'd better go. See you." With one last smile, Logan eased his way through the shifting mass of rugby players to grab the big white bag with his name scrawled on it. I noticed there was a smiley face drawn in the *O*—Simone's work, obviously.

Seconds later he was on his way out. I watched him go, feeling oddly disappointed. I figured it was probably because I hadn't learned more about his mother. It was always cool to hear about successful women in science. It gave me hope that my dreams of becoming a biomedical researcher someday could actually come true.

Simone made a beeline for me when I entered the kitchen. "Well?" she demanded. "Tell me everything!"

"Everything?" I grabbed an apron from the hook by the door and tied it around my waist. "That'll take a while."

"Ha-ha, very funny. You know what I mean." She jabbed

me in the arm with a latex-gloved finger. "Logan. You. What happened after I left? Did he ask you out?"

"What? No!" I shot a look at my dad and Uncle Rick to make sure they hadn't overheard. "Are you crazy?"

"Girls!" Uncle Rick's voice rang out from the other end of the huge stainless-steel table, where he was rapidly assembling a pair of roast-beef subs. "More work, less gossip, please."

"*You're* crazy if you missed the way Logan was checking you out," Simone hissed.

There was no more time for talking. Which was just as well, since I had no idea what to say to *that*.

Whenever anyone asked how Simone and I became best friends, I told them it worked on the same scientific principle as one of those school IDs that unlocked the gym doors when you held it close enough to the sensor. Proximity. We'd been friends since we were tiny tots because we lived right next door to each other.

Actually, that was only part of the reason. The other part was that our mothers had been best friends since they were teenagers themselves. I doubted they'd started out as different as Simone and me, but their lives had definitely gone in different directions for a while. My mom married her high school sweetheart, graduated from the local university, then went right to work in the family business (dragging Dad in with her). Meanwhile, Simone's mom went off to college in California. She spent her junior year abroad in Paris, then went back to France after she graduated. She lived there for a couple of years, and in the process fell madly in love with a Frenchman of Algerian descent. They got married, she dragged him back here to live, and the rest was history.

I'd always found that story awfully romantic, even though I wasn't usually the romantic type. I liked the idea that there really was a big, wide world out there beyond my boring little hometown. Anytime I doubted that, I just had to look at Simone's dad. Or, better yet, listen to him. Even after almost twenty years in the US, his accent was atrocious.

"*Bonjour*, Bailey," he greeted me when I let myself into the Amrou house through the screen door on Sunday evening. "Simone is in the kitchen helping to wash up after supper. Oh, and tell your mama that her apple pie was *délicieux*!" He kissed his fingertips, just like someone in a cheesy French film. Only he wasn't doing it ironically—he actually meant it. I loved when he did stuff like that, even though it embarrassed Simone sometimes.

"Thanks, Mr. A," I told him with a smile. "I'll tell her."

I headed toward the kitchen. Simone and I hadn't had much chance to talk since the rugby invasion earlier that day. First we'd both stayed busy making sandwiches and serving customers. Then Simone's mom had called to tell her to head home for dinner (and to bring a pie from the bakery case).

Simone heard me coming. "I thought you'd never get here!"

she complained, tossing aside the dishrag she was using to dry a pan. "Mom's forcing me to be her scullery maid."

"Her what?" I shot a look at Mrs. Amrou, who was dunking a pair of wine glasses into the sink. Simone and her mother didn't look much alike except for their matching sharp chins and tiny ears. Mrs. Amrou was petite and pale, with auburn hair and a smattering of freckles across her upturned nose.

"You'd better not complain about washing a few pots and pans, m'dear," Mrs. Amrou told her daughter. She glanced over at me and winked. "Otherwise I'm sure Bailey's folks could find you a nice full-time job washing up at Eats."

"Okay, okay." Simone set the pan on the drying rack. "But if Bails doesn't help me figure out how to pass this test tomorrow, that might be my only option for employment someday."

"Fine." Mrs. Amrou chuckled. "You're excused."

"Great." Simone grabbed a pair of sodas out of the fridge and tossed one to me. "It's a gorgeous night. Let's study in the tree house."

Soon we were climbing the rickety homemade ladder leading up to the tree house. It had been our spot since the third grade, when our dads had helped us build it. It was basically just a big wooden box tucked into a crook of the ancient oak that stood on the property line between our two houses, shading Mr. Amrou's hammock on their side and Mom's hostas on ours. When we were younger, Simone and I used to wait up there until her dad fell asleep in the hammock, then have contests to see who could drop a piece of popcorn or a potato chip or whatever and have it land on his face. Good times.

Simone dumped her books on the rough plank floor, then flopped onto one of the big overstuffed floor cushions we'd made in our eighth-grade family-science class (which didn't actually have much to do with science at all, by the way, unless you counted cooking and sewing as science, which I didn't).

"So," she said. "I've totally got the scoop on your new boyfriend."

"What?" I grabbed her biology textbook, flipping through it until I found the chapter on RNA. "Hey, aren't we supposed to be studying? You know, so you don't flunk out of bio class and become a professional dishwasher?"

"That can wait." Those three words pretty much summed up Simone's philosophy on life and homework, at least when boys were involved. "I texted the girls as soon as I could to see if any of them knew anything about Logan."

"The girls" were our other friends. Well, they'd started out as Simone's other friends, really. They were mostly like her— popular and confident and pretty. But they seemed to accept me as their token science-geek friend, so it all worked out.

"What did they say?" I couldn't help asking.

Simone's eyes lit up. "See? I *knew* you liked him!" she crowed. "I mean, since when do you care about the latest boy gossip? Even a super-hot, super-smart boy who was practically drooling all over you?"

"Give me a break," I muttered, folding a corner of a page up and down where Simone had dog-eared it. "If you don't want to tell me what you found out . . ."

"No, no, I'm telling you." She scrolled through her phone as she talked, checking her messages. "None of them knew a thing about him yet, but they were all intrigued."

A horrible thought occurred to me. "Wait. You didn't, like, tell them I'm madly in love with this guy or something, did you?"

"Of course not!" She sounded offended. "That's *your* news to share—when you're ready."

"Which will be approximately never," I said. "Because it's not true."

"Whatever you say." She smirked, then glanced down at her phone again. "Okay, so the only one who'd even vaguely heard about Logan was Taylor. She confirmed that he's a sophomore like us, only she thought he was a girl."

"She did?" That was pretty ditzy even for Taylor, who didn't always take in all of life's little details. She was actually pretty smart—she'd written a poem last year in English class that had ended up winning all sorts of awards and getting published in the university's literary magazine. But at times she seemed to be trying to live up to the dumb-blonde stereotype, even though her hair color came straight out of a bottle.

"Yeah. Apparently her mom mentioned there'd be a new kid starting in our class soon, but with all the background screaming, Taylor thought the name was Lauren or something, not Logan."

That made more sense. Taylor's mom worked in the front office at school, and Taylor had twin toddler half brothers who talked constantly and at the top of their lungs.

"What about Ling?" I asked. "Her dad must know Logan's mom, right? He's on the hiring committee at the university."

"Yeah, I thought of that too." Simone shrugged. "She was clueless, but promised to dig up the dirt."

I nodded. If there was any dirt to be dug up, Ling would find it. The girl could be relentless—verging on ruthless.

Simone peered at her phone's screen. "Wait, Megan just texted me back." She scanned the message. "She doesn't know anything about Logan. But she's dying to check him out."

"Yeah, I bet." Megan was one of the prettiest girls in school— and one of the most boy crazy.

Simone lowered her phone and eyed me. "Is that jealousy I sense over there?" she teased. "I knew it was love at first sight!"

"Don't be silly. There's no such thing." I hesitated. "Or at least, scientists say what most people call love at first sight is actually a mostly involuntary physiological reaction that comes from the release of adrenaline and dopamine and some other chemicals in the brain based on a quick assessment of a potential mate's facial features."

"Very romantic." Simone grinned. "Is all that mumbo gumbo true?"

"It's mumbo *jumbo*. And yes—I read an article about it in one of the science journals a couple of months ago."

"So is that how you felt when you first laid eyes on Logan?" She waggled her eyebrows. "Like you just really, really dug his facial features? Or what?"

"I don't know. It was weird."

"You're going to have to be more specific."

I picked at the edge of the textbook page, thinking back to seeing Logan walk in the door. "Usually I don't think about guys that much. I mean, what's the point?"

Simone sighed. "Not this again."

I shrugged. What could I say? She knew my philosophy about guys and dating. I'd always figured that logically, there wasn't much point in wasting time on high school romance. For one thing, most of the guys at school were much more interested in sports and movies and stuff than anything intellectual, including science. Meanwhile I was all about studying hard so I could get into a great college (preferably MIT, though I knew that was a long shot). Guys tended to find that weird, apparently, since they seemed to be in no hurry to ask me out.

But that was okay; I was in no hurry either. I figured I had much better odds of meeting a smart guy, one I had something in common with, once I got to college. Or if not there, then in med school for sure.

"Anyway, it doesn't matter," I told Simone, pushing her textbook toward her. "Guys like Logan don't notice me, remember? He was probably just being polite, maybe hoping I'd put in a good word for him with you."

"No way." Simone sounded sure of herself. "He barely looked at me."

"You're delusional." I chewed my lower lip thoughtfully. "I just wish I knew why I reacted that way to this particular guy. Maybe I'm deficient in iron or something. I've read that can cause mental confusion."

She ignored my hypothesis. "When did it start?" she asked. "You reacting to Logan, I mean. Was it as soon as he walked in the door?"

I thought about it for a second. "I think so. I definitely noticed right away that he was pretty cute. That's just neurotransmitters at work, though."

"What? Wait, never mind, don't start up with all that again." She leaned forward. "So then how did you feel?"

"Well . . . intrigued, I guess? Like I wanted him to come over and talk to us, but at the same time I wanted to run away and hide." I shook my head. "Totally illogical."

"And then when you were talking to him . . . ?"

"It was—mostly cool, I guess. I mean, you were there—you heard me spewing gibberish as usual. But he didn't laugh or roll his eyes or anything. He was actually pretty easy to talk to." I shrugged. "At least for a guy."

"I have a diagnosis for you, Dr. Myers." Simone leaned back against the tree house wall, looking very serious. "I'm afraid you've come down with a bad case of . . . sparks."

I wrinkled my nose. "What?"

"Sparks." She smiled. "That's when two people hit it off. You know—chemistry."

"We don't take that until next year," I joked weakly, glancing at her bio book. "Anyway, even if I do have a case of sparks, I'm sure it's totally one-sided."

"I don't think so. But how do you know until you go for it? What have you got to lose?"

Typical Simone. "Kind of a lot, really." I started ticking items off on my fingers. "My dignity, my self-respect, my lunch . . ."

"No, seriously. It's not like you're throwing yourself at some random guy. He was really into you. I guarantee it."

I thought about that for a second. Simone was really good at this boy-girl stuff. She'd had her first "date"—sharing a juice box with Zach Harasta—way back in first grade, and had never looked back. All our friends went to her for advice about guys. Whether they took that advice or not, Simone usually turned out to be right in the end. Could she be right about this?

"No way," I answered myself aloud. "We're making a mountain out of a molehill."

Simone chugged her soda. "We'll just have to see what happens at school tomorrow," she said, wiping her mouth. "And don't worry, I know you're new to this. I'll be with you every step of the way, helping you figure it out."

"Figure what out?" My little sister's face suddenly appeared over the lip of the tree house doorway. "What are you guys talking about?"

"Ash!" I scowled at her. "What are you doing here?"

She smirked. "Simone's mom sent me. I'm supposed to spy on you and see if you guys are studying or goofing off."

Simone rolled her eyes. "Great job, Jamesina Bond. You're super stealthy."

"Whatever." That was Ashley's favorite word lately. "So are you studying or what? I have to go back and tell her or she won't give me a piece of pie."

"Yes, we're studying." I grabbed Simone's textbook and flipped through the pages. "See? Study study study."

"Okay. See you." Ash's head disappeared. A moment later we heard a soft thump as she jumped the last few feet to the ground.

Simone checked her watch and gulped, suddenly looking panicky. "Oh, wow, it's getting late. We'd better start studying for real."

"Agreed." I plunked the textbook down in front of her. I was tired of thinking about the whole Logan encounter anyway—it made my head hurt. "Now, tell me what you know about RNA. . . ."